MONSIEUR LINH
AND HIS CHILD

Also by Philippe Claudel in English translation
Grey Souls (2005)
Brodeck's Report (2009)

PHILIPPE CLAUDEL

MONSIEUR LINH
AND HIS CHILD

Translated from the French by
Euan Cameron

MACLEHOSE PRESS
QUERCUS · LONDON

First published in Great Britain in 2011 by

MacLehose Press
an imprint of Quercus
21 Bloomsbury Square
London WC1A 2NS

First published in the French language as *La petite fille de Monsieur Linh*
Copyright © Éditions Stock, 2005
English translation copyright © 2011 by Euan Cameron

This book is supported by the French Ministry of Foreign Affairs, as part of the Burgess
programme run by the Cultural Department of the French Embassy in London

Liberté • Égalité • Fraternité
RÉPUBLIQUE FRANÇAISE

The moral right of Philippe Claudel to be
identified as the author of this work has been
asserted in accordance with the Copyright,
Designs and Patents Act, 1988

Euan Cameron asserts his moral right to be identified as
the translator of the work

A CIP catalogue record for this book is available from the British Library

ISBN 978 1 906694 99 9

10 9 8 7 6 5 4 3 2 1

Designed and typeset in Albertina by Libanus Press, Marlborough
Printed and bound in Great Britain by Clays Ltd, St Ives plc

To all the Monsieur Linhs of the earth
and to their little girls

For Nohm and Emélia

An old man is standing on the after-deck of a ship. In his arms he clasps a flimsy suitcase and a newborn baby, even lighter than the suitcase. The old man's name is Monsieur Linh. He is the only person who knows this is his name because all those who once knew it are dead.

Standing at the stern of the ship, he sees his homeland, the land of his ancestors and his dead ones, fading away into the distance, while in his arms the child sleeps. The land is growing fainter, it becomes infinitesimal, and Monsieur Linh watches it vanishing over the horizon, for hours, regardless of the wind that blows and ruffles him like a puppet.

The voyage lasts a long time. Days and nights. And the old man spends all this time on the after-deck of the ship, gazing at the white wake that eventually converges with the sky, peering at the horizon, still searching for the vanished shores.

When they want to make him go to his cabin, he allows himself to be guided without a word, but they find him again a little while later, on the after-deck, one hand holding the railing, the other clasping the child, with the small, worn leather suitcase lying at his feet.

A strap holds the suitcase together to prevent it coming apart, as if there were precious goods inside it. In actual fact, it merely contains old clothes, a photograph that is almost entirely faded by the sunlight, and a canvas bag into which the old man has sprinkled a fistful of earth. That was everything he was able to take with him. And the child, of course.

The child is well behaved. She is a girl. She was six weeks old when Monsieur Linh came on board with a countless number of other people similar to him, men and women who had lost everything, who had been hurriedly rounded up and who did as they were told.

Six weeks. This is how long the voyage lasts. So that when the ship arrives at its destination, the little girl has already doubled the length of her life. As for the old man, he feels as if he has aged a hundred years.

Occasionally, he hums a song to the little girl, always the same one, and he sees the baby's eyes open, and her mouth too. He watches her, and he observes much more than the face of a very young child. He sees landscapes, bright mornings, the slow and peaceful plod of the buffalo in the paddy fields, the bowed shadow of the giant banyan trees at the entrance to his village, the blue mist that comes down from the mountains towards evening, like a shawl that falls softly over one's shoulders.

The milk he is giving the child runs down the corners of her lips. Monsieur Linh is not used to this yet. He is clumsy. But the little girl does not cry. She goes back to sleep, and as for him, he continues to gaze out over the horizon, over the foam made by the wake, and into the far distance in which, for quite a long time now, he has no longer been able to discern anything.

Finally, one November day, the ship arrives at its destination, but the old man does not want to get off. Leaving the ship means leaving behind what still binds him to his homeland. Two women then lead him gently towards the quayside, as if he were unwell. It is very cold. The sky is overcast. Monsieur Linh breathes in the smell of the new land. He does not smell anything. There is no smell. It is a land without smell. He clasps the child more closely to him and he sings the song in her ear. Really he sings it for himself as well, so that he can hear his own voice and the music of his language.

Monsieur Linh and the child are not alone on the quayside. There are hundreds of people, like themselves. Old and young, waiting obediently, their meagre belongings alongside them, waiting in weather that is colder than any they have ever known, to be told where to go. No-one talks to anyone else. They are frail statues with sad faces, shivering in utter silence.

One of the women who had helped him leave the ship comes

up to him again. She indicates that he should follow her. He does not understand what she is saying, but he understands her gestures. He shows the child to the woman. She looks at it, appears to hesitate, and eventually smiles. He starts to walk and follows her.

The child's parents were Monsieur Linh's children. The child's father was his son. They died in the war that has been raging in his country for years now. They set off one morning to work in the paddy fields, with the child, and by the evening they had not returned. The old man ran. He was out of breath when he arrived at the rice field. It was nothing but a vast hole, bubbling with water, with the corpse of a disembowelled buffalo lying on one side of the crater, its yoke broken in two like a bit of straw. There was also his son's body, and his son's wife's body, and further away, the little girl, her eyes wide open, unharmed and wrapped in a blanket, and beside the child a doll, her own doll, the same size as her, which had had its head blown off by the blast of the bomb. The little girl was ten days old. Her parents had called her *Sang diû*, which in the local language means "mild morning". This was the name they had given her, and then they had died. Monsieur Linh had taken the child. He set off. He decided to leave for ever. For the child's sake.

When the old man thinks about the little girl in this way, it seems to him that she snuggles up even more closely to his side.

He grips the handle of his suitcase and follows the woman, his face glistening beneath the November rain.

On reaching a room that is pleasantly warm, the woman shows him to a seat. She makes him sit down. There are some tables, some chairs. It is very big. For the time being, they are on their own, but a little later all the people from the ship arrive and take their places. They are given some soup. He does not want to eat, but the woman comes up to him to make him understand that he must eat. She looks at the little girl who is asleep. He sees the way the woman looks at the child. He tells himself that she is right. He tells himself that he must eat, that he must build up his strength, for the child's sake if not for himself.

He will never forget the tastelessness of that first mouthful of soup, swallowed down half-heartedly, when he had just disembarked, when it was so cold outside, and when it was not his country outside, but a strange and foreign land, one that would always remain so for him, in spite of the time that would pass, in spite of the ever greater distance between his memories and the present.

The soup is like the air of the city that he breathed in as he left the ship. It does not really have any smell, not really any taste. There is nothing familiar about it. There is none of the delicious tang of lemongrass, the sweetness of fresh coriander, the smoothness of cooked tripe. The soup enters his mouth and passes into his body, and he is suddenly filled with all the strangeness of his new life.

In the evening, the woman takes Monsieur Linh and the child to a dormitory. The place is clean and spacious. Two families of refugees have already been living there for three weeks. They have made themselves comfortable and at home. They knew one another because both families came from the same southern province. They fled together, drifting for a long time on the wreckage of a boat, before being hoisted aboard a real ship. There are two men, both young. One of them has one wife, the other has two. The eleven children are noisy and happy. They all look at the old man as if he is a nuisance, and they stare in astonishment, and with slight hostility, at the baby he is carrying. Monsieur Linh feels as if he is disturbing them. Nevertheless, they make an effort to welcome him and they bow to him, calling him "Uncle", as is their custom. The children want to take little *Sang diû* in their arms, but he tells them calmly that he will not allow it. He presses her to him. The children shrug. The three women whisper to one another, then they turn away. The two men sit down again in a corner and get on with their game of mah-jong.

The old man looks at the bed that has been allocated to him. He puts the child gently down on the ground, removes the mattress from the base of the bed and places it on the floor. He lays the child on the mattress. Finally, he lies down beside her, fully dressed, holding the handle of his suitcase in his hand. He closes his eyes and forgets about the families who have sat down in a circle and are starting to eat. He closes his eyes and falls asleep dreaming of the fragrances of his native land.

Days go by. Monsieur Linh does not leave the dormitory. He devotes his time to looking after the child, going about his task in a manner that is both considerate and clumsy. The little girl does not complain. She never cries, and she does not scream very much. It is as if, in her own way, by holding back her tears and her imperious childish desires, she wants to help her grandfather. This is what the old man thinks. The children stare at him and often make fun of him, but without daring to do so aloud. The women also laugh sometimes as they watch him coping awkwardly when he changes her or washes her:

"Uncle, you haven't a clue! Let us do it! We won't harm her!"

And they laugh all the more. The children do too, even more loudly than their mothers. But every time he shakes his head and refuses their help. The men whisper to one another in a despondent way. They go back to their chatter and their games. Monsieur Linh could not care less about what they may think of him. Nothing else matters but his little girl. He wants to look after her in the best possible way. Often, he sings her the song.

The woman from the first day, the one he has privately nick-named "the woman from the quayside", comes to bring food each morning and to enquire about everyone's health. A girl comes with her. She knows the language they speak. She acts as an interpreter.

"Haven't you gone outside yet, Uncle? Why don't you go out? You should get some air!"

He says no, silently. He does not dare admit that he is fright-ened of going outside, of going out into this unknown city, in this unknown country, frightened of coming across men and women whose faces he does not know and whose language he does not understand.

The interpreter girl looks at the child, then speaks at some length to the woman from the quayside. The woman replies to her. They have a discussion. The girl carries on with what she was saying.

"The little creature will waste away if you don't take her for walks! Look, Uncle, her skin is so pale, she looks almost like a young ghost . . ."

The girl's words make him anxious. He does not like ghosts. There are too many of them already who come to haunt him at night. He clasps *Sang diû* a little closer to him, and he promises to take her for a walk the next day, if the weather is not too cold.

"The cold here, Uncle," the young woman says to him, "is like the warm rains at home, you'll have to get used to it."

The woman from the quayside goes off with the interpreter girl. Monsieur Linh bids them goodbye ceremoniously, as he always does.

The following day, he emerges from the dormitory for the first time and goes outside. There is a wind, a wind that blows in from the sea and leaves a trace of salt on the lips. The old man lets his tongue run over his lips so that he can taste the salt. He has put on all the clothes which the woman from the quayside had given him the day after he had arrived. He is wearing a shirt, three pullovers, a woollen coat that is a little too big for him, a raincoat, as well as a cap with ear-flaps. Thus attired, he looks like some sort of large puffed-up scarecrow. He has also dressed the child in all the clothes that he asked the woman from the quayside for her. One would think he was carrying an enormous oblong-shaped balloon in his arms.

"Don't get lost, Uncle, it's a big city!" the women called out to him when he was getting ready to go out. They said this with a laugh.

"Be careful they don't steal the child from you!" one of them went on. At this they all laughed, the women, their sons and their daughters. Looking up, the men did so too. They laughed seeing him dressed up like this and one of them called out, through the acrid fumes of the cigarettes they both smoked continuously as they played: "If you haven't come back within a year, we'll inform the Refugee Bureau!" He bid them farewell and he went outside, terrified by what the women had just said about children who are kidnapped.

Monsieur Linh walked straight ahead, never changing pavements. He told himself that if he never changed pavements and did not cross any roads, he could not get lost. He would just have to retrace his steps to find the building where the dormitory was. So he walks straight ahead, holding the child tightly to him, the child that has suddenly become enormous because of all the clothes that swathe her body. The cold lends colour to her cheeks that protrude from the woollen jumpers: very soon the little girl has the complexion of a beautiful and delicate rose that reminds him of water-lily buds, the ones that open out in the ponds at the very beginning of spring. His own eyes are streaming. The cold brings tears to his eyes, which he allows to drop down his face and is unable to wipe away because he is holding his little girl in both his hands, so that no thief can steal her from him.

He proceeds along the pavement without really noticing the city, he is so busy concentrating on his own footsteps. The woman from the quayside and the interpreter girl were right. It is true that it does one good to move about a bit and walk, and the child who looks at him with her tiny eyes that gleam like precious black stones seems to think so too.

Monsieur Linh goes on walking like this for a long time, scarcely realising that he is continually passing in front of the building where the dormitory is, for since he never strays from the pavement, his circular walk simply takes him on a circuit of the block.

After about an hour, he feels tired and sits down on a bench, opposite a park on the other side of the road. He sits the little girl on his lap and takes out of his pocket an envelope into which he has deposited some cooked rice. He puts the rice in his mouth, chews it to make it creamier, like baby food, then he removes it from his mouth and gives it to the child. He then lets his eyes roam all around him.

Nothing is like anything he knows. It is like being born a second time. Cars go by that he has never seen before, endless numbers of them, in a steady, well-ordered stream. On the pavements, men and women walk along very quickly, as if their lives depended on it. No-one is dressed in rags and tatters. No-one begs. Nobody pays any attention to anyone else. There are also many shops. Their large and spacious windows brim with goods that the old man never even knew existed. Looking at them makes him feel giddy. He thinks back to his village rather as one thinks of a dream one has had and which one is not quite sure whether it really is a dream or lost reality.

In his village, there was only one street. Just one. The ground consisted of mud. When the rain fell, violent and vertical, the street became a raging stream in which naked children chased one another about, laughing. When the weather was dry, the pigs slept there, sprawling in the dust, while the dogs rushed hither and thither, barking. Everyone knew one another in the village, and everyone greeted each other as they passed. There were twelve families in all, and each of these families knew all about the others and could name the grandparents, the ancestors, the cousins, and knew what possessions each of them owned. The village was really like one large family, divided up among houses that were built on stilts, beneath which chickens and ducks cackled and rooted about in the earth. The old man is aware that when he talks to himself about his village, he does so in the past tense. The thought plucks at his heartstrings. He really does feel his heart being torn apart, so he presses his free hand tightly to his chest, where the heart is, to make the pain stop.

Monsieur Linh does not feel cold sitting on the bench. Thinking of his village, even in the past, is a little like still being there, although he knows that nothing of it remains, that all the houses have been burned down and destroyed, that the animals are dead, the dogs, pigs, ducks, chickens, as well as most of the people, and those who have survived have left for the four corners of the earth, as he has done. He lifts the collar of his raincoat and strokes the forehead of the sleeping child. He wipes away the rice that has spilled here and there over the little girl's mouth.

He notices all of a sudden that they are not alone on the bench: a man has sat down and is looking at him and looking at the little girl too. He is probably the same age as Monsieur Linh, though perhaps not quite as old. He is taller, stockier, and he is wearing fewer clothes. The man gives a slight smile.

"Not warm, is it?"

He blows on his hands, takes a pack of cigarettes out of one of his pockets, and taps the bottom of the pack with a precise gesture that makes a cigarette pop out. He holds out the pack to Monsieur Linh, who shakes his head.

"You're right," the man says, "I ought to stop . . . But what with all the things one ought to stop doing!"

He places the cigarette between his lips, in a simple and smooth motion. He lights it, inhales the first puff deeply, and closes his eyes.

"It's good all the same . . ." he murmurs eventually.

The old man does not understand anything the man who has

just sat down is saying. Nevertheless, he senses that the words are not unfriendly.

"Do you come here often?" the man goes on. But he doesn't seem to expect a reply. He inhales the smoke of his cigarette as if he were savouring each puff. He goes on talking, without actually looking at Monsieur Linh.

"I come almost every day. It's not that it's very pretty, but the place appeals to me, it brings back memories."

He stops talking and glances at the child on the old man's lap, then he looks at the old man huddled up in his layers of clothing, and then back again at the child's face:

"A pretty little dolly you've got there. What's her name?" He points at the child with his finger as he speaks, lifting his chin in a questioning manner. Monsieur Linh understands.

"*Sang diû*," he says.

"*Sans dieu . . .,*" the man continues, 'that's a funny sort of name. Mine is Bark, and you are?" and he proffers his hand.

"*Tao-laï*," says Monsieur Linh, following the polite convention used in the language of his native land to say good-day to someone. And he clasps his companion's hand in both of his. A giant's hand, with enormous, callused fingers that are cracked and badly chapped.

"Well then, good-day, Monsieur Tao-Laï," says the man, smiling at him.

15

"*Tao-laï*," says the old man once more as the two of them go on shaking hands for some time.

The sun breaks through the clouds. This does not mean the sky is no longer grey, but it is a grey that reveals patches of white at dizzying heights. Monsieur Bark's smoke seems to want to catch up with the sky. It escapes from his lips, and then rises up very quickly. Sometimes, he breathes it out through his nose. This reminds Monsieur Linh of buffalos' nostrils, of fires too, lit in the forest in the evening in order to keep the wild animals away, and which gradually peter out during the hours of darkness.

"My wife is dead," Monsieur Bark says, as he crushes the butt of his cigarette on the pavement with the heel of his shoe. "Two months ago. Two months, that's both a long time, and a very short time as well. I don't exactly know how to measure time any more. However much I say to myself 'two months'; 'two months', that is to say eight weeks, which is to say fifty-six days, it no longer means anything to me."

He takes out his pack of cigarettes once more, offers another one to the old man – who, with a smile, refuses again – then he places it between his lips, lights it, and inhales his first puff with his eyes closed.

"She used to work across the road, in the Park. She had a merry-go-round – you're bound to have seen it before – with little wooden horses made of polished wood. An old-fashioned merry-go-round, there are hardly any of them left."

Monsieur Bark stops speaking. He smokes in silence. Monsieur Linh waits for his voice to come back. Although he does not know the meaning of the words spoken by this man who has been sitting beside him for several minutes, he is aware that he likes the sound of his voice, the deep tone of this voice, its solemn power. He may also like the sound of this voice precisely because he is unable to understand the words it utters, and is therefore sure that they will not hurt him, they will not say what he does not wish to hear, they will not ask painful questions, they will not go back into the past in order to resurrect it brutally and hurl it at his feet like a bloody corpse. He looks at his companion, while at the same time clasping the child on his lap to him.

"You are probably married, or have been, I don't wish to pry," Monsieur Bark continues. "But you must understand me. I always used to wait for her on this bench. She closed her merry-go-round at five o'clock in winter, at seven in summer. I would see her from the other side of the street when she left the Park. She would wave at me. I would give a wave back. But I'm boring you, forgive me . . ."

As he speaks these words, Monsieur Bark puts his hand on Monsieur Linh's shoulder. Through the numerous layers of clothes, the old man can feel the grip of the thick hand, which lingers there for a while. He does not dare move. All of a sudden, a thought comes to his mind, like a razor. Supposing this man were a kidnapper, as the women in the dormitory had said? He shivers. He clasps the child to him very tightly. His face must have betrayed his fear, for Monsieur Bark realises that something has just occurred. He is embarrassed and removes his hand from the shoulder.

"Yes, forgive me, I talk and talk, it's just that I talk so seldom these days . . . I shall leave you in peace."

And he gets to his feet. Immediately, Monsieur Linh's heart beats more slowly and calms down. A smile returns to his face and his hands loosen their grip on the little girl's body. He is annoyed with himself for having thought badly about this man whose expression is at once sad and warm-hearted. Monsieur Bark doffs his hat.

"Goodbye, Monsieur Tao-laï, don't be angry with me for all the things I've told you . . . Until we meet again perhaps!"

Monsieur Linh bows three times and clasps the hand Monsieur Bark extends to him. He watches him walk away up until the moment when Monsieur Bark becomes lost in the crowd, a peaceful crowd that makes no noise, no commotion and that wends its way, fluid and gnarled like a huge sea monster.

The following day, the old man leaves the dormitory at the same time. He is wearing what he wore yesterday. He has dressed the little girl in the same way too. The women and the children made fun of him again. The men, for their part, did not even look up. They were too busy playing their game.

Sometimes, the men quarrel. One accuses the other of cheating. Voices rise. Counters and coins fly around. Then everything suddenly quietens down. They smoke cigarettes that leave a grey haze in the dormitory, with a strong and irritating smell.

During the mornings, the dormitory is quiet, for the three wives go out with their children. The children start to take over the city. They come back with words Monsieur Linh does not understand, and they bawl them out at the top of their voices in the dormitory. In their arms the women are carrying the goods they went to collect from the Refugee Bureau, then they prepare the meal. There is always a portion for Monsieur Linh. Tradition requires it. Monsieur Linh is the eldest. He is an old man. It is a duty for the women to feed him. He knows this. He knows very well that they do not do this out of kindness or out of love. What is more, when one or other of them brings him his bowl, she makes a face that does not deceive him. She places the bowl in front of him, turns around, and walks away without saying a word. He thanks her with a bow, but she does not even notice what he is doing.

He is never hungry. Were he on his own, he would not eat. Besides, if he had been on his own, he would not even be there, in this land which is not his own. He would have remained in his own country. He would not have left the ruins of the village. He would have died at the same time as the village did. But there is the child, his little girl. And so he forces himself to eat even though the food in his mouth tastes like cardboard, and when he swallows it, it makes him feel sick.

Monsieur Linh walks cautiously along the pavement. The child he is carrying does not stir. She is peaceful, she always is. Peaceful like the morning when he awakes, and the night, which had wrapped his village, the paddy fields and the forest in its cloak of darkness, is gently dispersed.

The old man moves onwards with small steps. It is just as cold as it was yesterday, but his many pieces of clothing protect him. Only his eyes, his mouth and the tip of his nose grow numb in the biting cold. The crowd is still just as large. Where can all these people be going? Monsieur Linh does not really dare look at them.

He keeps his eyes lowered to the ground. He only looks up from time to time, and then he sees faces, an ocean of faces, coming towards him; they pass him by, they brush against him, but none of these faces takes any notice of him, and still less of the child that lies in his arms.

All these women, all these men, Monsieur Linh has never seen so many. There were so few people living in the village. Occasionally, of course, he went to the market in the small regional town, but there too he knew everyone. The peasants who came to sell their goods, or else to buy them, lived in other villages similar to his own, between rice fields and forests, on the slopes of mountains whose summits were rarely seen because they were generally plumed in mist. They were related to one another by more or less distant bonds of kinship, by marriages or by cousinhood. There was much chatter at the market. They laughed. They told one another about who had died, their news, their stories. You could sit on stools belonging to the little mobile restaurants and have some bindweed soup, or a sticky rice-cake. The men told tales about hunting, they talked about crops. The younger ones looked at the girls, who would suddenly blush and whisper in one another's ears as they rolled their eyes.

Thinking of this, Monsieur Linh finds himself dreaming. But he collides unexpectedly with something that nearly causes him to fall. He lurches. The child! The child! He hugs little *Sang diû* to him with all his strength. Slowly he recovers his balance. His old heart thumps in his chest. It is going to break. Monsieur Linh looks up. A fat woman is talking to him. Or rather, yelling. She is much bigger than him. Her face is unpleasant. She shakes her head, she frowns. The crowd goes by, without taking any notice of what her angry voice is saying. The crowd goes by, like a herd that is blind and deaf.

Monsieur Linh bows to the fat woman several times to make her understand that he is sorry. The woman walks away, grumbling and shrugging her shoulders. The old man can hear his heart pounding. He speaks to it as if it were an animal at bay. He tries to soothe it. The heart seems to understand. It beats more slowly. It is like a dog settling down in front of the entrance to the house after having barked in fear upon hearing the thunder and the storm.

Monsieur Linh looks at his little girl. She has not woken up. She has not noticed anything. The collision has simply caused the bonnet and the hood that protect her to come adrift. The old man adjusts her clothing. He strokes the child's forehead. He whispers the song to her. He knows that she can hear it, even in her sleep. It is a very old song. Monsieur Linh heard it sung by his grandmother, who in turn knew it from her own grandmother. It is a song that comes from the mists of time, and which the women sing to all the little girls in the village when they are born, and have done so since the village first existed. This is what the song says:

> *Always there is the morning*
> *Always the light returns*
> *Always there is another day*
> *One day it's you who will be a mother.*

The words come to Monsieur Linh's lips, his old, thin, cracked lips. And the words are a balm that soothes his lips, as well as his soul. The words of the song make light of time, place and age. Thanks to them, it is easy to go back to where you were born, to where you lived, to the bamboo house with its lattice-work floor, permeated with the smell of the fires over which the meal is cooked, while the rain drips its clear and liquid coating on the roof made of leaves.

The song does the old man good. He forgets the cold and also the fat woman he bumped into with his head down. He goes on walking. Taking small strides. As if he were gliding over the ground. He has already been round the block twice and he can feel himself growing weary. The cold air penetrates his throat and gives him a burning sensation, but he is surprised to find that it is not really so unpleasant.

When he breathes in, on the other hand, he does not experience anything. This country definitely does not smell of anything, nothing either familiar or sweet. Yet the sea is not far away. Monsieur Linh knows this. In his mind's eye he sees once more the ship aboard which he arrived, the big port lined with huge cranes that dug down into the heavy bellies of the ships as if to dismember them. But however much he breathes in, closes his eyes and breathes in again, he cannot catch the smell of the sea, that mixture of heat, salted meat and fish left out in the sun which is the only smell of the sea he has ever known, on the day he had had to walk as far as the coast, two days away from the village, in order to search for an elderly, half-crazy aunt who had got lost there. Monsieur Linh smiles at the memory of his aunt, of her toothless mouth, of her eyes burned by the sun, this woman who lived on the fringes of life and who used to look at the sea and speak to it as if she were a parent: "There you are, you see, I've found you at last, I told you I would, it's pointless trying to hide now!"

The aunt had set off from the village a week earlier. She had wandered among the rice fields for days and nights. She had slept there and her hair was covered in mud. Her clothing had become torn by brambles along the way. She looked what she had become: a mad woman, old and exhausted, who talked to the sea and who had had to be taken by the hand and brought back to the village, and throughout that entire journey she had droned on, uttering curses and greetings, mistaking the peasant women she encountered for nymphs, and the men, bent beneath their bamboo yokes, for evil spirits.

Monsieur Linh was strong in those days. Throughout almost the whole of the journey home he had carried his aunt on his back. All his muscles bulged on his body. He had powerful arms, easily able to stop a buffalo by gripping it by the horns. His legs were powerful too, and he would propel himself with a swivel of the hips to deliver a blow to his opponents when he wrestled with them at the village fair. It was a long time ago. *Sang diû* was not born, of course. Neither was *Sang diû*'s father, his son. Monsieur Linh was still a young man who had not taken a wife and, as he passed by, the girls used to turn and twitter to one another in the way birds do in springtime.

Nowadays, Monsieur Linh is old, and weary. The strange land exhausts him. Death exhausts him. It has fed on him in the way eager young goats suckle their mother, forcing her to lie on her side because she cannot continue. Death has taken everything from him. He has nothing left. He is thousands of kilometres from a village that no longer exists, thousand of kilometres from the empty tombs of the corpses who died only a few feet away from them. He is thousands of days away from a life that was once beautiful and delightful.

Without realising, Monsieur Linh has just laid his hand on the bench opposite the Park. The one where he had sat and taken a rest the previous day. The one where that rather plump, kindly and smiling man had placed his hand on his shoulder. He sits down, and all of a sudden the memory of that man comes back to him, of his mouth which seemed to devour the cigarettes, of his eyes that were at once serious and laughing, of his tuneful voice that uttered words he did not understand, and also the memory of the weight of his hand, when he placed it on his shoulder, and he flinched in fear, before feeling ashamed at having reacted in that way.

Yes, it was just here, Monsieur Linh tells himself as he settles the child on his lap after sitting down on the bench. The little girl had opened her eyes. Her grandfather smiles at her. "I am your grandfather," Monsieur Linh tells her, "and we are together, there are two of us, the only two, the last two. But don't be afraid, I am here, nothing can happen to you. I am old, but I'll still have enough strength, as long as it is needed, as long as you are a little green mango in need of an old mango tree."

The old man looks at *Sang diû*'s eyes. They are the eyes of his son, they are the eyes of his son's wife, and they are the eyes of his son's mother, his dearly beloved wife, whose face is always present within him like a delicately drawn painting, embellished with wonderful colours. Come on now, there's his heart beating too fiercely again, at the memory of his wife, even though she departed so long ago, when he was a young man, when his son was barely three years old and did not yet know how to tend the pigs or bind the sheaves of rice.

She had very big eyes – a brown that was almost black – fringed with lashes as long as palm leaves, and fine, silky hair which she plaited as soon as she had washed it in the spring. When she walked along the mud paths – which were scarcely wider than two hands held side by side and ran between the rice fields – carrying a bowl full of doughnuts on her head, her body fired the imaginations of the boys who tilled the ground buried beneath the muddy water. She laughed at them all, innocently, but it was Monsieur Linh who had married her, and it was to him that she bore a beautiful boy, before dying from a nasty fever, or possibly from a spell cast by a jealous and barren woman who had once lusted after Monsieur Linh.

The old man thinks of all this. Sitting on this bench which, within the space of just two days, has become a familiar little s pot, a chunk of floating wood he could cling to in the midst of a strange, broad, swirling torrent. And nestling cosily against him he clasps the last twig of the branch, sleeping its fearless sleep for the time being, without melancholy or sadness; that sleep of a satisfied infant, happy to have found the warmth of the skin it loves, its pleasant smoothness and the caress of a loving voice.

"Good-day, Monsieur Tao-laï!"

Monsieur Linh gives a start. Standing beside him is the fat man who had spoken to him the previous day. He is smiling at him.

"Bark, Monsieur Bark, do you remember?" the man repeats as he holds out his hand in a gesture of friendly greeting.

Monsieur Linh smiles, makes sure the little girl is lying safely on his lap, and extends both his hands towards the man as he says *"Tao-laï!"*

"Yes, I remember," says the man, "Tao-laï, that's your name. Mine, as I said to you before, is Bark."

Monsieur Linh smiles. He did not expect to see the man again. He feels pleased. It is like finding a signpost on a path when you are lost in the forest and have been wandering around for days without recognising anything. He makes a little space so as to indicate to the man that he can sit down, and this is what he does, he sits down. Straightaway, he fumbles in his pockets, brings out a pack of cigarettes and offers one to Monsieur Linh.

"Still not? You're quite right."

And he puts one between his lips, which look thick and tired. Tired lips, Monsieur Linh tells himself, have no meaning, and yet that is what they are. It is as if the man's lips are tired, tired because of a heavy and insoluble sadness.

Monsieur Bark lights the cigarette, which sparkles in the cold air. He closes his eyes, inhales his first puff, smiles, and then looks at the little creature Monsieur Linh is clasping on his knees. He looks at her and smiles even more, a kindly smile. He nods his head, as if giving his approval. Monsieur Linh suddenly feels proud, proud of his little girl who is nestling against him. He lifts her up a little so that Monsieur Bark can see her better, then he smiles at him.

"Look at them rushing along!" Monsieur Bark says, pointing to the crowd, while the spiralling smoke from his cigarette drifts into his face and makes him screw up his eyes.

"They are in such a hurry to get there . . . And to get where, I ask you! The place where we shall all go one day! I can't help thinking of such things when I see them like that . . ."

He drops his cigarette butt and its red embers spatter the ground with a few sparks that are very quickly extinguished. He crushes the butt very carefully with his heel. All that remains is a black smear of ashes and a few tiny shreds of tobacco and paper that very quickly absorb the damp from the ground and flutter a little, as if gasping for their last breath.

"Have you noticed that they're almost all going in the same direction?" says Monsieur Bark, already placing another cigarette between his lips and using a lighter whose flame is so feeble that the tobacco barely catches.

Once again, Monsieur Linh is lulled by the voice of this stranger, although rather less of a stranger than he was the previous day, who talks to him without his being able to take in a word of what he is saying.

Occasionally, some of the smoke from his cigarette reaches the old man's nostrils, and he finds himself inhaling this smoke, trying to breathe as much of it as possible inside him. It is not really that he finds the smoke pleasant – the smoke from the cigarettes in the dormitory is horrible – but this kind is different, it has a good smell, a perfume, the first that the new country has given him, and this perfume reminds him of the pipes which the men from the village lit in the evenings, sitting outside their houses, while the indefatigable children played in the street, and the women sang as they wove the bamboo.

Monsieur Bark has large fingers, the first and second of which have taken on an orange-yellow colour from holding the many cigarettes that he smokes continuously. Monsieur Linh looks across at the Park, on the other side of the street. He can see mothers with lots of children going in there. Further away, he can make out ponds and large trees, what appear to be cages too, possibly intended for large animals, possibly for animals from his homeland. And then it occurs to him that this is his own fate, that he is inside an immense cage, without bars or a keeper,but one that he will never be able to get out of again.

Seeing that Monsieur Linh is staring at the entrance to the Park, Monsieur Bark points to it with his finger.

"It's another world over there, the people don't run. It's only the children who run, but with them it's not the same thing, they laugh as they run. Not at all the same thing. You should have seen the smiles on the merry-go-round! On my wife's wooden horses! What smiles! And yet, when you think about it, a merry-go-round is just a circle that goes round and round, so why should the children enjoy it so much . . . I was always touched watching it, watching my wife operating the merry-go-round, knowing that her job was to make children happy."

When Monsieur Bark speaks, Monsieur Linh listens to him very attentively and looks at him, as if he understood everything and did not want to lose any of the meaning of the words. What the old man senses is that the tone of Monsieur Bark's voice denotes sadness, a deep melancholy, a sort of wound the voice accentuates, which accompanies it beyond words and language, something that infuses it just as the sap infuses a tree without one seeing it.

And suddenly, without really thinking about it, and astonished by what he is doing, Monsieur Linh places his left hand on Monsieur Bark's shoulder, just as the latter had done to him the day before, and at the same time he looks at him and smiles. The man returns his smile.

"I talk and talk . . . What a chatter-box, eh? You're very kind to put up with me. It does me good to talk, you know! We talked a lot, my wife and I . . ."

He remains silent for a moment, time enough to drop his cigarette butt on the ground and to crush it with the same deliberation, take out another cigarette, light it, close his eyes, and savour the first puff.

"We'd thought of leaving as soon as she retired. She had a year to go. But for her, abandoning her merry-go-round like that was out of the question, she wanted to find someone to take it over, someone suitable, she was fussy, she did not want to hand it over to just anyone. It was a bit like her child, the merry-go-round, the child we never had."

The fat man's eyes gleam very brightly. Probably the cold, Monsieur Linh reckons, or the smoke from the cigarette.

"We didn't want to stay here, we'd never liked this city; I don't know whether you yourself like it, but we could never bear it. So we thought of finding a little house, inland from here, in a village, no matter which, in the middle of the fields, near the forests and a river, a small village, if they still exist, where everyone knows one another and says hello. Not like here. That was our dream . . . Are you leaving already?"

Monsieur Linh has got to his feet. He has just realised it is late and that he has not put anything in his pockets with which to feed his little girl. He has to get back before she wakes up. Before she cries because she is hungry. She never cries, but precisely because of this Monsieur Linh hopes that it will always be thus, that as long as he is able to look after her, as long as he is there for her, ready to anticipate all her wishes and to dispel all her fears, she will never cry.

Monsieur Bark looks at him with sadness and disbelief. Monsieur Linh realises that he is surprised, and probably disappointed too, so he gesticulates with his head at the sleeping child.

"*Sans dieu* . . ." says Monsieur Bark with a smile. Monsieur Linh nods.

"Very well, goodbye Monsieur Tao-laï! Until the next time!"

The old man bows three times to say goodbye to Monsieur Bark, and, since the latter is unable to shake Monsieur Linh's hand because he is clasping his little girl to him, he places his hand on the old man's shoulder, firmly, and with warmth.

Monsieur Linh smiles. It is all he wanted.

When he arrives at the dormitory, the woman from the quayside is there, waiting for him, together with the interpreter girl. They were worried that he had not come back. This is what the girl tells him. Monsieur Linh explains about his walk. He also speaks of the bench, and the fat man on the bench. They are relieved. The woman from the quayside asks him whether everything is alright, whether there is anything he needs. Monsieur Linh is about to say no, but he changes his mind and asks the girl whether he is entitled to cigarettes. Yes, he would very much like some cigarettes.

"I didn't know you smoked, Uncle," says the girl. And she translates. The woman from the quayside smiles at him as she listens. It's agreed, he will have one pack of cigarettes per day.

Just as they are getting ready to leave, the woman from the quayside suddenly begins a long conversation with the girl. The latter nods from time to time. She turns to Monsieur Linh and says to him:

"Uncle, you won't be able to stay here in the dormitory for

ever. It's a temporary solution. The Refugee Bureau will soon examine your case, as it does everyone's. You will see people who will ask you questions, a doctor too. Don't worry, I'll be there with you. Afterwards, they will suggest something permanent, and a place will be found where you can be more peaceful. Everything will be alright."

Monsieur Linh listens to the girl. He does not know what to say to her, so he says nothing. He does not dare. He does not tell her that in spite of the families he feels quite happy in this dormitory, that the little girl has got used to it and seems to like it there. Instead of all that, he asks a question, just one: he asks the girl how one says "good-day" in the language of this country. The young interpreter tells him. He repeats the word several times, so as to fix it in his memory. He closes his eyes so as to concentrate. When he opens them again, the two women are looking at one another and smiling. Monsieur Linh then asks the girl which province she was born in. "I was born here," she says, "I was in my mother's womb when my parents arrived on a ship, like you."

The old man remains open-mouthed, as if someone had told him about a miracle. For him, being born here makes no sense. He then asks the girl what her first name is. "Sara," she replies. Monsieur Linh frowns. He does not know this name. "And what does your name mean?" he enquires. "It means Sara, Uncle, that's all. Nothing else." The old man nods. He says to himself that a country where names do not mean anything is a very strange country.

The two women are by the door. They hold out their hands to him. Monsieur Linh clasps their hands, then bows, holding the still sleeping child against his breast. He must now think about feeding her. He walks over towards the corner of the dormitory that is allocated to him. He lays *Sang diû* on the mattress. He undresses her. She opens her eyes. He hums the song to her. Then he dresses her in light clothes, a cotton blouse, which she wore at home. The blouse has lost its colour. Monsieur Linh washes it every morning and hangs it up by the radiator. By the evening, the blouse is dry.

The old man takes off the layers of clothing he is wearing. He folds the clothes, one by one, except for the overcoat which serves as extra covering during the night, for he is always worried that the child might be cold.

The families are eating in a circle, ten yards away from him. Most of the children have their backs to him, as do the women. From time to time the two men glance up at him before returning to their food, which they gobble down. All that can be heard is the noise made by their tongues, the chopsticks and their mouths. Beside the mattress, Monsieur Linh finds a bowl of rice, some vermicelli soup and a piece of fish. He says thank you and bows twice. No-one is taking notice of him any longer.

He chews the rice into a small pulp that is not too thick and gives it to his little girl. He gives her the soup to drink from a spoon, having blown on it for a long time so that the broth does not burn her delicate lips. He crumbles a little fish too, which he slips into her mouth, but very soon she appears to be full and does not swallow it. She is sleepy already, Monsieur Linh thinks. He remembers that years ago he used to watch his wife going through the same motions to feed their son, the son who is now dead. He thinks of his wife's gentle movements, and it is from that very memory that the old man derives the knowledge and the words that enable him to look after *Sang diû*.

The two men have carried on with their games of mah-jong. They pour themselves small glasses of rice beer which they drink in a single gulp. The women wash the bowls, plates and sauce-pans. The children squabble. The younger ones yawn and rub their eyes.

Monsieur Linh lies down on the mattress, wraps his very scrawny arms around his little girl, closes his eyes and joins her in sleep.

The following day is brighter. The white sunlight nips the sky. It is colder too. Monsieur Linh is walking along the pavement, wrapped up in all his clothes, and carrying his child, of course. He has slipped the packet of cigarettes he was given this morning into the pocket of his overcoat. It was one of the women from the dormitory who brought it at the same time as the food which she had gone to collect from the Refugee Bureau, as she did each day. "It's for you apparently, Uncle," she had said. She had handed him the packet with a shrug. The two men who were resting from their night spent playing games and were dozing on their mattresses made some comments in a low voice, then they were silent.

The pack of cigarettes makes a small lump which the old man can feel as he walks along. Merely feeling this small lump makes him smile. He is thinking of the expression on the fat man's face when he offers him the pack.

Monsieur Linh doesn't walk several times round the block. He goes directly to the bench and he sits down. It is pleasant to be sitting there, on this very bright day, on this bench, and to be waiting. The crowd does not move at the same pace as it does on other days. It is still just as dense, but the people are not walking as quickly. They are in small groups and appear to Monsieur Linh to be expensively dressed. They are conversing with one another, many of them are laughing and their faces look relaxed. They seem to be relishing the day and the moment. There are children with them who occasionally, when they notice the old man on the bench, point their fingers at him and laugh. The parents then take them by the hand and drag them further away. Some of them try to get closer to him and to the little girl on his lap, to get a better look at her no doubt, but once again the parents catch hold of them and drag them off by the arm.

"Do I frighten them?" Monsieur Linh wonders. Then he tries to look at himself, and all he sees is a large ball of wool, padded and shapeless, made up of scarves, a cap, a coat and jumpers.

"I probably do frighten them. They must take me for a wicked genie disguised as an old man." This notion amuses Monsieur Linh.

Opposite him, on the other side of the street, families in their hundreds hurry to the entrance to the Park, while others are leaving it. They form two noisy and colourful streams that mingle and sometimes scurry about in large eddies, similar to those that spring up, in the rainy season, on the River of Sorrows,

40

whose waters rumble not far from the village.

It gets its name from the legend that tells of a woman who, wishing to bathe her children, lost all seven of them on the same day. And ever since, if you sit on the bank and listen, on certain evenings you can hear the sound of sobbing rise up from the river into which the woman, inconsolable at the death of her little ones, eventually threw herself.

But it is a legend that is only told, in the evening by the fireside, in order to frighten the children so that they should be careful not to drown themselves, for in actual fact it is a beautiful river with clear waters and plenty of fish, in which it is good to cool oneself. You can find freshwater shrimps there and the little crabs that are then grilled on the embers. The men bring the buffalo to drink there. The women wash their clothes in it and also their long hair which, when it floats in the water, looks like black, silken seaweed. The bamboo dips its roots there while waiting to be dried. The river is the colour of the trees that are reflected in it, and their roots plunge down to the river-bed so as to draw up the cool water. Green and yellow birds skim its surface. They are like arrows of light, unfathomable, almost dreamlike.

Monsieur Linh opens his eyes once more. One day, he must tell *Sang diû* about all this, tell her about the river, the village, the forest, about her father's strength and her mother's smile.

The old man looks at the entrance to the Park again. He would very much like to go and see what it is that is so marvellous over there, and what makes the families hurry along there like this. But it is on the other side of the street, and this vast, wide street is always teeming with cars shooting past, cars that never stop going up and down, at full speed, in both directions, amid a roar of horns and a fog of blue and grey smoke.

Time passes. Monsieur Linh can measure this by the cold that penetrates his shoes, his three pairs of socks, and reaches his feet. Time goes by, and he is still alone on the bench. The fat man is not coming. Perhaps he does not come every day. Perhaps he will never come again?

Monsieur Linh can feel the pack of cigarettes in his coat pocket. The small lump now prompts an immense sadness within him. He recalls the touch of the old man's hand when he placed it on his shoulder. He then remembers that he is alone in the world, with his little girl. Alone together. That his country is far away. That his country is no longer there, so to speak. That it is nothing but fragments of memories and dreams that survive only in his weary old man's head.

The day is drawing to a close. In the distance, the sun seems to be falling heavily in the sky. He must go back. The fat man has not come. Monsieur Linh sets off, his pack of cigarettes in his pocket, and on his lips the word that means "good-day", and which he has not uttered.

The old man sleeps badly. He has the feeling that he is frozen with cold. He convinces himself that all his clothes have been stolen, that he has nothing any more, that he does not even have his suitcase which contains the bag of earth and the photograph with the faded image. He tosses and turns, then, shortly before dawn, a heavy sleep eventually sweeps him into a dark and bottomless well.

When he wakes up, it is late. Immediately, he senses that something is not normal. He reaches out his hand, does not find anything and sits bolt upright, looking to the right and to the left: "*Sang diû! Sang diû!*" Monsieur Linh's cries have caused the women, who are squatting in a circle around a bowl, peeling vegetables, to turn around. Their husbands are snoring. "*Sang diû! Sang diû!*" the distraught old man continues to moan as he springs to his feet and hears his bones cracking in his body and his heart thumping.

Suddenly, at the far end of the dormitory, he catches sight of three of the children, the youngest ones. They are laughing. They are laughing out loud. And who does he see is with them? His little girl, whom they are passing from hand to hand, not taking any care, not being gentle; his distraught little girl whose eyes open and close continuously. Monsieur Linh leaps to his feet, he crosses the dormitory and rushes over to the children.

"Stop it! Stop it! You're going to hurt her, she's still too little to be with you!"

He takes *Sang diû* in his arms, strokes her, soothes her, comforts her. He is shaking all over. He was so frightened.

As he goes back to the corner of the dormitory where his mattress is, he walks past the women. One of them says to him:

"They're children, Uncle, they're allowed to play among themselves, why don't you just let them be?"

Monsieur Linh hugs his little girl to him, tightly, very tightly. He does not answer them. The woman looks at him with an expression of disgust. "Crazy old man," she mutters between her teeth. A little later, in order not to have to come near him, the same woman will toss the pack of cigarettes to him. The old man will quickly put it into the pocket of his overcoat, next to the other one.

Monsieur Linh is late going out that day. He stays lying despondently on his mattress for a long time, while *Sang diû* goes back to sleep. He does not touch the food which one of the two other women has put down beside him.

All of a sudden, the dormitory is filled with loud shouts, and the two men who were playing cards are arguing vehemently. They are standing up and confronting one another like fighting cocks. One accuses the other of cheating. They grab each other. The three women seem frightened as they look on. Monsieur Linh does not want his little girl to see any of this. Swiftly, he gets her ready, dresses himself and puts on all the layers of woollens, then he leaves at the moment that one of the men, his eyes filled with fury, is brandishing a knife beneath the nose of the other.

Outside, the weather is grey. A fine, freezing rain is falling, of the kind that greeted them on the first day, when they disembarked from the ship. The very low sky seems to want to crush the city. Monsieur Linh pulls down the bonnet over the child's head. One can hardly see her. He pulls up his own collar.

The crowd on the pavement has begun its frenetic race once more. There are no longer any families strolling along, no more men and women gazing into the air and smiling. People are walking quickly, their heads bowed. In their midst, Monsieur Linh resembles the trunk of a small, dead tree carried away on the current, and which is swept along and tossed about by the waters without his being able to do anything about it.

"Monsieur Tao-laï! Monsieur Tao-laï!"

As if in a dream, the old man hears a warm, hoarse voice twice bidding him good-day. Then all of a sudden he realises that the voice does not belong to a dream, but comes from behind him, and the moment he grasps this, he recognises the voice. So at the risk of being jostled, he stops walking, turns around and notices one raised arm waving at him from ten yards away, and then another, and the voice continues and calls out good-day to him twice more.

Monsieur Linh smiles. It is as if the daylight were dispelling his low spirits. Within a very few seconds, Monsieur Bark is alongside him, all breathless, with a broad smile on his face. The old man closes his eyes, searches his memory for the word the interpreter girl had taught him and, looking at Monsieur Bark, says in a loud voice:

"Good-day!"

Monsieur Bark is finding it hard to recover his breath. He has run too far. Monsieur Linh can smell the aroma of the tobacco on his breath. The fat man smiles at him:

"I'm really pleased to see you! But come on, let's not stay here, we'll catch our death in this rain."

And, without asking the old man's consent, he drags him off to an unknown destination. Monsieur Linh allows himself to be led. He is happy. He would follow the fat man anywhere. He can feel the two packs of cigarettes in his pocket and that makes him smile even more. He is no longer cold. He forgets the dormitory, the unpleasant women, the two men who were quarrelling. There he is, walking along, his little girl pressed tightly to him, beside a man who is much taller than him, who must weigh twice as much, and who never stops smoking.

Monsieur Bark pushes open the door to the café and lets Monsieur Linh in. He selects a table, in a corner, and signals to the old man to sit on the wall seat while he takes the chair.

"What weather! I can't wait for it to be fine again!" Monsieur

Bark says, rubbing his hands together and lighting another cigarette. He inhales the first puff in the way he always does, closing his eyes for a few seconds. He looks at the child and smiles. "*Sans dieu!*" he says. Monsieur Linh nods his head and gazes at the little girl whom he has placed on the bench next to him and who closed her eyes when he laid her down. "*Sang diû . . .*" he says again, proudly, because he thinks that she is very beautiful, that she looks like his son, like his son's wife, and through her he traces the likeness back to the beloved image of his own wife.

"I shall order," says Monsieur Bark, "otherwise we shall never be served! Trust me, Monsieur Tao-laï, in weather like this I know what we need to warm ourselves! Alright?"

Monsieur Linh does not know why the fat man keeps saying good-day to him, but he says it so gently and with such kindness that he finds it delightful. Without knowing what he meant, he realises that he was asking him a question, so he gives a faint nod of his head, as if to say yes.

"That's that, then!" Monsieur Bark gets up and walks over to the counter. He gives the order to the barman. Hastily, the old man takes the opportunity to bring out the two packs of cigarettes and to place them on the table, next to the fat man's lighter, a metal lighter, heavily dented, as if it had received plenty of knocks. Monsieur Bark remains at the bar for a while. He is waiting for the drinks. This allows Monsieur Linh to see him from the back for the first time: he has slightly stooped shoulders, like those who have carried heavy loads on their yokes all their lives. Perhaps that is his job, he thinks, carrying yokes filled with bricks, plaster, or earth.

Monsieur Bark's voice rouses him from his thoughts:

"Watch out there, excuse me!" He is carrying two cups that are steaming and that give off a strange smell, both lemon-scented and sensual. He puts them on the table, and he sits down. Because he is so busy being careful not to spill the drinks, and not to burn himself either, Monsieur Bark has not yet noticed the two packs of cigarettes in front of him. When he sees them, the first thing that occurs to him is that someone has left them behind by mistake. He starts to turn round, then he stops, for he has just understood. He looks at the old man, who smiles mischievously.

It is the first time in a long while that anyone has given Monsieur Bark a present. His wife often used to give him little things: a pen, a tie, a handkerchief, a purse. He gave her little things, too: a rose, some scent, a scarf, outside the usual occasions. It was a sort of game between them.

He takes the two packs of cigarettes in his hand. He feels greatly moved on account of these two simple packs of cigarettes, a brand he does not care for as it happens, and which he never smokes because they have a menthol smell he cannot bear. But this is of no importance. He looks at the two packs, looks at the old man opposite him. He feels a sudden urge to embrace him. He cannot find the words because they are rather jumbled up. He clears his throat and simply says:

"Thank you . . . thank you, Monsieur Tao-laï, you are too kind. I'm so pleased, so very pleased."

Monsieur Linh is happy because he senses that the fat man is too. And so, since it seems that in this country people say good-day frequently, Monsieur Linh says good-day once more to Monsieur Bark, pronouncing the word as the young interpreter had taught him.

"You're right," Monsieur Bark now replies. "It is a good day!" And with his plump fingers he removes the cellophane wrapping from one of the packs, pulls out the sheet of silver paper, taps the bottom of the pack, offers a cigarette to Monsieur Linh who refuses with a smile, smiles himself as if he were saying "Still not?", slips one between his lips, lights it with his battered lighter, inhales the first puff, and closes his eyes.

And because it is the old man who has given him these cigarettes, he suddenly finds them much better than he remembers them. Yes, much better. It's actually very pleasant, this aroma of mint. Monsieur Bark has the feeling of becoming much lighter. He has the feeling that his lungs are expanding, that the air is getting into them more easily. He relaxes. It is nice in this café.

This is what Monsieur Linh feels too. It is nice here. There is hardly anyone around. There are just the two of them. The child is sleeping. It is as if she were in a bed. Everything is fine.

"But come on now, drink. Drink it. If you don't drink it hot there's no point!"

Monsieur Bark shows how to do it. He takes the cup between both his hands, blows on the liquid several times and sips a mouthful, making a sort of whistling sound. The old man tries to imitate him: he takes hold of the cup, blows, sips, whistles, but suddenly he is overcome with a fit of coughing.

"Ah, it's strong stuff! But it will warm you up, you'll see! The secret is that it's got to be boiling when it's served: boiling water, sugar, lemon, and a good shot of alcohol, any kind, whatever you have to hand! It's not that difficult!"

Monsieur Linh has never drunk anything remotely like this concoction. He recognises the taste of lemon well enough, but otherwise, everything is new. What is especially new is that as he takes little sips and feels his stomach burn with a continuous fire, a strange drowsiness comes over him and makes him sway about on the wall seat.

The fat man's face is flushed. His red cheeks are like paper lanterns. He appears to enjoy the cigarettes that Monsieur Linh has given him, for he never stops smoking them, lighting the next one with what remains of the one before.

The old man opens his overcoat, and also unbuttons his

raincoat, and then he laughs for no reason. He can feel his face burning him. His head is spinning a little too.

"So, we are feeling better, aren't we?" Monsieur Bark says to him. "We used to come here with my wife, in wintertime. It's quiet. There's not too much noise . . ."

But all of a sudden, he becomes gloomy. His laughter fades, like a fire upon which a handful of soil has been thrown. He fiddles with his almost empty cup in which the slice of lemon has sunk. His eyes glisten. He slumps forward. He says nothing. He even forgets to light another cigarette. It is the barman who rouses him. He is going off duty and would like to close the till. Monsieur Bark fumbles in his pockets and draws out a few coins which he gives to the man.

Monsieur Linh looks at him and smiles.

"Life's grim at times, eh?" Monsieur Bark says to him.

The old man does not say anything and continues to smile at him. Then, as if impelled by an urge he is unable to control, he starts to hum:

Always there is the morning . . .

He hums the song in his native tongue, which gives the words a delicate, syncopated, slightly muffled musical sound:

Always the light returns
Always there is another day . . .

Monsieur Bark listens to him. The music envelops him.

One day it is you who will be a mother.

Monsieur Linh stops singing. What can he be thinking of? Why sing the song to the fat man? Why hum him these words which he cannot understand? He suddenly feels ashamed, but he sees that Monsieur Bark is looking at him and appears to be happy once more.

"It's beautiful, Monsieur Tao-laï, it's very beautiful, even when you can't understand the words. Thank you."

The old man gently picks up the child who is still asleep and who barely opens her eyes when he presses her to him. He stands up and bows to Monsieur Bark.

"That was a lovely moment," the man says to him. "It did me good."

"Good-day," says Monsieur Linh.

"Well, goodbye, Monsieur Tao-laï," Monsieur Bark says. "Until tomorrow, I hope."

The old man bows twice. The fat man puts his hand on his shoulder. Monsieur Linh is leaving, but just as he is about to walk through the door of the café, he hears Monsieur Bark calling out to him, "And thanks for the cigarettes!", as he holds the two packs aloft.

The old man smiles, nods, and goes out.

The fresh air lashes his face. The walk stretches his old legs. He feels very heavy and very light at the same time. He has a slight headache. There is a strange taste in his mouth, but he is happy, happy to have seen the fat man and to have shared some time with him, while the child rested.

When he pushes open the door to the dormitory, dusk has already fallen outside. The two men are playing cards in silence. They glance at him, a weary, lifeless glance that takes nothing in, as if he no longer existed. As for the women, they do not turn round. Neither do the children.

Monsieur Linh undresses the little girl. He washes her carefully, and puts on her cotton blouse. Then he gives her a little rice, some milk, and a little mashed banana too. The old man is not hungry. He undresses and lies down beside the child who is already asleep. He thinks again of the fat man, of his smile of surprise when he realised that it was he, Monsieur Linh, who had brought him the cigarettes. He closes his eyes. He reflects on the taste of that boiling, lemon-scented drink he shared with him.

He falls into a heavy slumber.

Monsieur Linh and Monsieur Bark meet every day. When the weather allows, they stay out of doors, sitting on the bench. When it rains, they return to the café and Monsieur Bark orders the strange drink, which they consume holding the cups between their hands.

From now on, as soon as he wakes up, the old man looks forward to the moment when he will go to meet his friend. He refers to him as "his friend" in his mind, because that is what he really is. The fat man has become his friend, even though Monsieur Linh does not speak his language, even though he does not understand it, even though the only word that he uses is "Good-day". It is not important. In any case, the fat man himself only knows one word of Monsieur Linh's language, and it is the same word.

Thanks to Monsieur Bark, the new country has a face, a way of walking, a solidity, a weariness and a smile, an aroma too, that of cigarette smoke. Without realising it, Monsieur Bark has given all this to Monsieur Linh.

Sang diû has got used to these meetings, to Monsieur Bark's warm breath, to his powerful hands striated with cracks, to his big, calloused fingers. Sometimes, when Monsieur Bark senses that the old man is growing weary, he carries her. The little girl makes no fuss. It is funny to see her in the fat man's arms. He is so big and so strong that nothing can happen to the child. Monsieur Linh is calm. A kidnapper would not dare take on such a big, strong man.

Monsieur Bark still smokes just as much, perhaps even more, were that possible. But he now only smokes menthol cigarettes, which to his mind are excellent. When Monsieur Linh produces the pack to give to him, there is always a slight tremor inside him, a pleasant sensation that causes something to churn in his stomach a little and rise up into his throat. Then he smiles at the old man, thanks him, opens the pack straightaway, taps it at one end and extracts a cigarette.

Sometimes, the two of them stroll around the streets. Not just along one street any more, but along various streets, for Monsieur Bark walks all over the city with Monsieur Linh, introducing him to other districts, squares, avenues, narrow lanes, places that are deserted, and others that are full of shops where people go in and out like bees at a hive.

People stare at this curious couple, the old man who is so small and who seems so vulnerable, dressed in his multiple layers of clothing, and this giant of a man, puffing away like a steam engine; and then people turn their gaze to *Sang diû*, Monsieur Linh's pride and joy, whom he holds in his arms like a treasured possession.

When the stares become a little too hostile or intrusive, Monsieur Bark stares back at the curious onlooker, frowns and hardens his features. Then people may take him for someone very unpleasant. This amuses Monsieur Linh. The person who is being a nuisance drops his gaze and goes on his way. Monsieur Bark and Monsieur Linh laugh heartily.

One day, at the café, as they are enjoying the drink that always makes the old man's head spin a little, and which leaves him feeling warm and languorous, just as when one has a temperature and knows that it heralds an illness that is not very serious, Monsieur Linh pulls from his pocket the photograph, the only one he has ever had in his life. He had taken it out of his suitcase in the morning to show to his friend. He hands it to Monsieur Bark, who realises that it is important. He takes the photograph in his enormous fingers with great delicacy. He looks at it.

To begin with, he does not see anything, so faded and blurred is the image, lost in the years and the rays of sunlight. Then he eventually makes out a young man standing in front of a curious house that looks light and flimsy and is built on wooden struts, and next to this man, a woman, probably younger than the man, who is very beautiful, and whose flowing hair is gathered in a long plait. The man and the woman are looking straight at the photographer. They are not smiling and are holding themselves somewhat stiffly, as if they were frightened or overcome by the occasion.

When Monsieur Bark examines the man's face more closely, he discovers that it is unquestionably Monsieur Linh, who is sitting opposite him. It is the very same face, the same eyes, the same shape of mouth, the same forehead, but thirty, possibly forty years ago. Looking at the woman again, he then realises that he is gazing at Monsieur Linh's wife who, like his own wife, is probably dead since he has never seen her with him. So Monsieur Bark contemplates the features of this woman who is young – so young – and of a beauty that is at once sleek and mysterious, mysterious perhaps precisely because it is sleek and unaffected, and possessed of a disturbing and innocent simplicity.

Monsieur Bark puts the photograph down carefully in front of him, fumbles in the inside pocket of his coat, grabs hold of his wallet, which he opens and in turn takes out a photograph, one of his own wife, who is smiling as she tilts her head slightly to the left.

All that can be seen is the face, a full, round, slightly pale face, with red delineated lips, and large eyes that are creased due to her smile and probably because the sun is in her eyes. Behind the face, everything is green. It may be foliage. Monsieur Linh tries to recognise these leaves, to discover what tree they come from, but he cannot identify them. They do not have these types of leaves in his country. The woman appears to be happy. She is plump and happy. She must be the fat man's wife. The old man has never seen her. She works all the time. Or rather . . . yes, that must be it, she is dead. She is in the land of the dead, like his own wife, and perhaps, Monsieur Linh tells himself, perhaps in that far-away land his own wife and the fat man's wife have met one another, just as they themselves have met. The thought touches him. The thought pleases him. He hopes that this has happened.

The little girl is asleep on the seat. Monsieur Bark lights another cigarette. His eyes are shining brightly. Monsieur Linh starts to hum the song. For a while, they both remain like this, with the photographs next to the empty cups, laid out in front of them.

When they leave the café, Monsieur Bark takes Monsieur Linh by the shoulder and, as he does every day now, he accompanies him to the door of the building where the dormitory is situated. And once they are there, the two men spend a long time taking leave of one another as they say "Good-day".

In the dormitory, life has not changed. The two families are still there. The men spend their days and part of their nights playing cards or mah-jong, endlessly talking, laughing, insulting one another, and making up by drinking glasses of rice beer until they are often drunk.

The elder children are going to school now. They return with more and more words of the language of their country of exile. They teach these to the younger ones. The three women attend to the food and the washing. Monsieur Linh always finds his meal beside his mattress. He thanks them with a bow. Nobody takes any notice of him any more, nor does anyone speak to him. But he does not care. He is not alone. There is *Sang diû*. And there is the fat man, his friend.

One day, Monsieur Bark takes Monsieur Linh to the coast. It is the first time since his arrival, a few months ago, that he has seen the sea again. The fat man has taken him to the harbour, not to the place where he disembarked, that vast dock cluttered with cranes, unloaded cargo, waiting trucks and gaping warehouses, but somewhere quieter, in the shape of a bay, where the water and the fishing boats look as if they form part of a brightly coloured painting.

The two friends walk a short way along the quayside and sit down on a bench. They face the sea. Winter is over. The sun is warmer. Up above in the sky, a flock of birds swirl and sometimes dive into the harbour waters to emerge again with silvery slivers of fish in their beaks. Fishermen are repairing nets on their moored boats. Some are whistling. Others are talking in loud voices, calling out to one another and laughing. It is a very pleasant spot. Monsieur Linh inhales the air. He inhales deeply, with his eyes closed. Yes, he was not mistaken. There are fragrances here, real fragrances: of salt, of air, of dried fish, tar, seaweed and water. How good they are! It is the first time that this land has really smelled of anything, that it has had a tang. The old man is intoxicated by it. He thanks his friend from the bottom of his heart for having introduced him to this place.

Monsieur Linh takes off some of his little girl's clothes. He places her between himself and the fat man. Sitting up. The child opens her eyes. Her eyes meet the sea, the wide, open sea. The old man gazes out over it too. He can see himself on the ship once more, and images suddenly come back to him – terrible, loathsome and wonderful – and jostle about inside him. It is as if he were being pummelled with blows, striking at his heart, his soul, his belly and all his limbs. Yes, beyond the sea, far beyond it, days and days away, there is all that. There *had been* all that.

Then Monsieur Linh raises his hand, points his finger at the sea, the open sea, the blue and white horizon, and in a loud voice he utters the name of his homeland.

Monsieur Bark, who is also looking in the same direction, can then feel sudden bursts of fire pulsating and rushing through his veins, and images – terrible, loathsome and inhuman – come back to him too. In a loud voice, he also utters the name of the country that lies beyond the sea, Monsieur Linh's homeland. He says the name several times, in an increasingly muted tone, as his shoulders slump, as his whole body slumps, as he forgets everything, as he forgets even to light another cigarette, even though he has just dropped the stub of the previous one on the ground, without crushing it with his heel as he normally does.

Monsieur Bark is nothing but a fat, stooped man, who feebly repeats the name of Monsieur Linh's country, as if it were a litany, while his eyes fill with tears that he does not even attempt to hide or wipe away with his hands, and these tears pour down his cheeks, making his chin and neck wet, and drip down into the collar of his shirt where his skin absorbs them.

The old man notices. He puts his hand on his friend's shoulder and strokes it gently. Then Monsieur Bark stops looking out to sea, and through his tear-filled gaze looks at him instead.

"I know your country, Monsieur Tao-laï, I know it . . ." Monsieur Bark starts to say, and his loud voice is nothing more than a thin reed, tense, weak and ready to crack.

"Yes, I know it," he goes on, looking out over the sea and into the distance once more. "I went there a long time ago. I didn't dare tell you. I wasn't asked for my consent, you know. I was forced to go. I was young. I didn't know. It was a war. Not the one there is now, another one. One of the others. To think that your country is dogged by all the wars . . ."

Monsieur Bark stops speaking for a moment. His tears flow freely.

"I was twenty. What does one know at the age of twenty? I knew nothing. I had nothing in my head. Nothing. I was still just a big kid. A kid. And they put a gun in my hands when I was still virtually a child. I've seen your country, Monsieur Tao-laï, oh yes, I've seen it, I remember as if I had left it yesterday, everything has stayed in my mind, the smells, the colours, the rains, the forests, the laughter of the children, and their cries too."

Monsieur Bark turns his moist eyes to the sky. He sniffs loudly.

"When I arrived, when I saw all that, I thought to myself that this is what paradise must be like, even though I didn't really believe in paradise any more. And we were asked to bring death to this paradise, with our guns, our bombs, our grenades . . ."

Monsieur Linh listens to the fat man who is quietly addressing

63

him, as his tears stream from his eyes. The old man listens attentively, searching in the inflections of his voice for signs, for the beginning of a story and a meaning, a familiar tone. He thinks of the photograph his friend showed him a few weeks ago: the photograph of the plump, smiling woman. He also thinks of the strange merry-go-round they both went to see in the Park earlier, constantly spinning round and round. There were lots of wooden horses hanging from poles. The merry-go-round rotated. The horses went up and then down. The children who rode on them were laughing and making signs to their parents. There was loud and joyful music. The fat man had pointed to every part of the merry-go-round, chatting all the while. Apparently he liked this merry-go-round very much and knew it well. Monsieur Linh did not know why, but he had listened to him attentively, occasionally nodding his head. *Sang diû* seemed happy in his arms. The merry-go-round was a fine sight. In the end, the fat man went and shook hands with the person who operated it. They exchanged a few words together, and then he and Monsieur Linh had left the Park. The fat man did not speak for a long while afterwards.

Monsieur Linh observes his friend weeping and talking. He becomes convinced that the woman in the photograph and the merry-go-round with the wooden horses are part of the fat man's former life, and that it is this lost part of his existence which is now suddenly surfacing as they sit there by the sea, on this already sunny and almost mild day.

"All those villages we passed through, in the jungle, those people who lived on nothing and whom we had to shoot at; those very flimsy houses, built of straw and wood, just like your photograph, you know ... The fire in those houses, the shouting, the children who ran off down the tracks, naked, in the night and the flames ..."

Monsieur Bark stops speaking. He is still weeping. He feels sick. A sickness that comes from very far away and that troubles him, buffets him, beats away at him and crushes him. Shame haunts him like spleen.

"I ask your forgiveness, Monsieur Tao-laï ... for everything I've done to your country, to your people. I was only a kid, a wretched jerk of a kid, who shot, who destroyed, who probably killed ... I'm a shit, a real shit ..."

Monsieur Linh looks at his friend. A huge endless sob overwhelms him, as if it had sprung from the last word he has just uttered. It does not abate. The fat man's entire body shudders as if it were a ship blown off course by a storm. Monsieur Linh tries to put his arm around his friend's shoulder, without managing to do so because his arm is too small for this big shoulder. He smiles at him. He does his best to express a great deal in this smile, more things than any word could ever contain. Then he turns towards the open sea, making the fat man understand that he, too, must look over there, into the very far distance, and then, in a voice that is not sad but full of joy, Monsieur Linh repeats the name of his country, which suddenly rings out like hope and no longer like sorrow, before clasping his friend in both his arms, and feeling *Sang diû*'s body between them, protected and not crushed by their own bodies.

Three days later, Monsieur Bark invites Monsieur Linh to a restaurant. It is an imposing place, with lots of tables and lots of waiters. Monsieur Bark invites his friend to sit down and Monsieur Linh gazes around in astonishment. The old man has never seen anything so splendid. Monsieur Bark requests an additional chair and they sit *Sang diû* upon it. He then speaks to a man wearing black and white, and strangely attired, who jots things down in a notebook, bows and goes away.

"You'll see, we're going to enjoy ourselves, Monsieur Tao-laï!"

Monsieur Bark ties around his neck the large white napkin which lay next to his plate.

Monsieur Linh does the same. Afterwards, he ties another napkin around the small neck of the child, who waits, like a good girl, on her chair, not uttering a word.

"I used to come here sometimes with my wife," Monsieur Bark says. "When we wanted to give ourselves a little treat . . ."

His voice drops. There is a silence. He starts to speak again, but more slowly. Sometimes he breaks off for a moment, as if he were searching deep within himself for the words and was having difficulty finding them.

He is walking along a troubling path, Monsieur Linh tells himself. He listens to the fat man's voice, this voice that is so familiar to him even if it says things he never understands. His friend's voice is deep and hoarse; it seems to be negotiating stones and enormous rocks, like the streams that gush down the mountains before reaching the valley, making itself heard, laughing, weeping at times, and talking loudly. It is a music that embraces everything in life, its caresses as well as its struggles.

Monsieur Bark is silent. His head drops back. He passes his heavy hand over his forehead. He looks at the clouds through the bay window of the restaurant.

"How big the sky is . . ." he murmurs.

He turns towards his friend again and in a solemn voice says to him:

"I'm really glad to be here with you, Monsieur Tao-laï."

The waiter returns with the dishes. Monsieur Bark has ordered the very best. Nothing is too good. He remembers the afternoon by the harbour, how he poured out his whole heart to him, and also the old man's reactions, once he had stopped talking and was feeling upset and ashamed. You could not put a price on that.

Monsieur Bark and Monsieur Linh eat and drink. Monsieur Linh samples dishes he never knew existed. He is not familiar with any of them, but everything is very good. He drinks small sips of the wine that the fat man pours for him. His head feels a little hot. The tables sway. He laughs. Occasionally, he tries to make his child try one of the dishes, but she is not very hungry. She is always well behaved, but she is not swallowing her food. Monsieur Bark watches what he does with a smile. The other guests turn around sometimes and stare at them. Monsieur Bark could not care less.

After the dessert course, once the waiter has cleared the table, the fat man bends over and picks up a bag that he had placed beside him earlier when he had sat down, and he brings out a pretty packet which he hands to Monsieur Linh.

"A present!" he says. And since the old man hesitates, he continues: "Yes, go on, it's a present for you, Monsieur Tao-laï. Take it, please."

Monsieur Linh takes the packet. He is trembling. He is not used to presents.

"Well, open it!" says Monsieur Bark, motioning with his hands as he speaks.

The old man gently removes the wrapping paper. This takes time because he unwraps it meticulously and his fingers are not very agile. Once the paper has been taken off, he has a lovely box in his hands.

"Go on, go on!" The fat man laughs as he watches him.

Monsieur Linh opens the lid of the box. Inside, there is a thin sheet of very soft silky paper. He removes it. His heart is pounding. He lets out a little gasp. A princess' dress has just appeared, delicate, sumptuous and folded with great care. A dazzling dress. A dress for *Sang diû*!

"She's going to look beautiful!" says Monsieur Bark, as he glances across at the little girl. Monsieur Linh hardly dares touch the dress with his fingers. He is too frightened of damaging it. He has never seen such a beautiful piece of clothing. And the fat man has just given this dress to his child. Monsieur Linh's lips are affected by a nervous spasm, which he cannot control. He puts the dress back in the box, covers it with the tissue paper, and replaces the lid. He takes Monsieur Bark's hands in his and he clasps them firmly. Very firmly. For a long while. He takes *Sang diû* in his arms. Monsieur Linh's eyes gleam, he looks at his friend, he looks at the little girl, and his frail voice, slightly worn and quavering, then rises up in the restaurant:

> *Always there is the morning*
> *Always the light returns*
> *Always there is another day*
> *One day it is you who will be a mother.*

The song is over. Monsieur Linh bows towards Monsieur Bark, as if to thank him.

"Thank you, Monsieur Tao-laï," says the fat man.

In the late afternoon Monsieur Bark takes Monsieur Linh back. It is a pleasant day. It is not cold. Winter is over. When they reach the building in which the dormitory is situated, the two men take their leave of one another, as they do every evening: Monsieur Bark says goodbye to Monsieur "Good-day". Monsieur Linh says "good-day" to Monsieur Bark.

And, feeling happy, the old man goes upstairs to the dormitory, clasping his little girl to him.

The following day, the woman from the quayside arrives in the dormitory with the interpreter girl just as Monsieur Linh was getting ready to go out and join his friend. They have come to collect him. He must go with them. He has to see a doctor. They had forewarned him. It's the normal procedure. He would then have to accompany them to the Refugee Bureau to fill in certain documents.

Monsieur Linh is annoyed, but he doesn't dare let them know this. What will Monsieur Bark think? But the women are already dragging him away with them.

"May I bring my little girl?" he asks the interpreter girl. She translates for the woman from the quayside. She in turn looks at the child, demurs, and says something in reply. "No problem, Uncle!" the girl translates. Monsieur Linh tells her that in that case he needs a few minutes to dress her. A doctor is an important person. They need to make a good impression on him. The old man takes the box which his friend had given him. He takes out the beautiful dress and puts it on *Sang diû*. She looks wonderful.

She really does look like a young princess. The two women look on with a smile. The young children from the dormitory have come up to have a closer view of the dress, but their mothers call them back in an unpleasant tone of voice.

A car takes them through streets he has never seen. It is the first time that Monsieur Linh has travelled in a car. He is frightened. He cowers in the corner of the seat and clutches his little girl to his chest. She does not seem anxious. Her beautiful dress glistens in the reflections of the daylight. Why does the car go so quickly? What is the purpose? Monsieur Linh remembers the rhythm of the carts drawn by the buffalo, the long, smooth, swaying movement that sometimes caused you to fall asleep and sometimes to dream, and the landscape that changed with a precious slowness, a slowness that allowed you to look properly at the world, the fields, the forests, the rivers, and to talk to the people you came across, to hear their voices, to exchange news with them. The car is like a chest hurled from the top of a bridge. You suffocate inside it. All you can hear is a muffled roaring sound. The landscape spins by outside. You can't take any of it in. You have the impression that you are soon going to crash.

The doctor is a tall young man. The woman from the quayside goes into the surgery with Monsieur Linh. So does the girl. The woman from the quayside speaks to the doctor, and then she leaves. The girl stays behind to interpret. The doctor looks at the child in the old man's arms and asks the girl questions. She answers him. The doctor nods his head. He asks other questions, which the girl translates:

"Uncle, how old are you?"

"I am old," Monsieur Linh replies, "very old. I was born in the year of the tornado that devastated the village."

"You don't know how old you are?" asks the girl in amazement.

"I know that I am old, that's all. Knowing my age would not make any difference to me."

The girl speaks to the doctor, who makes a few notes. The questions continue. The girl translates them. Has Monsieur Linh already had an operation? In his homeland, did he have a doctor? Did he take any regular treatment? Does he suffer from high blood-pressure? From diabetes? Does he have any problems with his hearing? With his sight?

The old man understands half of what the girl is saying to him. He looks at her in amazement.

"You don't know my country," he says to her eventually. "The only doctor I ever saw was a very long time ago, when the army needed me. Otherwise, we looked after ourselves in the village. If the illness was benign, we got better. If it was malignant, we died. That's all there is to it."

The girl translates for the doctor, who says a few words. The girl tells Monsieur Linh that he wants to examine him. He will have to undress. She will stay behind the partition.

The old man entrusts *Sang diû* to her. He passes her gently into the arms of the girl, who takes her carefully and makes a kind comment about the dress. Monsieur Linh is touched. He thinks of the fat man, his friend.

The doctor examines him. He places his hands on his emaciated body with its smooth brown skin. He makes him open his mouth, he looks into his eyes and his nose, he puts strange instruments on his chest and around his arms, he taps his knees with a small hammer, he examines his stomach. He indicates to him that he may get dressed.

When he walks back towards the girl, he sees that the doctor is sitting down and writing on a sheet of paper. This goes on for quite a long time, and then he stands up. The girl says: "It's all done, Uncle, we can leave." She starts to guide him towards the exit. Monsieur Linh stops her and says to her: "But the little girl, the doctor didn't even look at the little girl."

The interpreter doesn't answer. She seems to be thinking. Then she speaks to the doctor. He agrees. "He'll look at her, Uncle, you're quite right to have asked."

The old man removes *Sang diû*'s beautiful dress and passes the child to the doctor, who takes her and lies her down on the examination table. The little girl doesn't utter a sound. Monsieur Linh talks to reassure her. The doctor goes about his work calmly and does not alarm the child. He inspects her eyes and her ears, he listens to her chest and places his hands on her tummy. He turns around, smiles at the old man, and speaks to the girl.

"The doctor says that she is in perfect health, Uncle, there's nothing you need worry about. He also said that she was a beautiful baby."

Monsieur Linh smiles. He is happy and proud. He dresses the child. The dress is soft to the touch and as soft as skin.

It is quite late when the two women take him back to the dormitory. It has been dark for a long time. There's no question of going out. Monsieur Bark must have left the bench anyway. He must be puzzled. He must be worried.

Before leaving, the girl says this to him:

"Tomorrow we're coming to collect you, Uncle. This is your last night here. We're going to take you to a place where you'll be far better off, much quieter and more comfortable."

Monsieur Linh feels desperate.

"I'm fine here, I don't want to leave . . ."

The girl translates for the woman from the quayside. They talk among themselves for a few seconds.

"There's no alternative," the girl says. "Everyone will be leaving, in any case, for the dormitory is closing down soon. And you won't be very far away. You're not going to another city."

This last remark reassures the old man somewhat. He will

remain in the city. So he will be able to go on seeing his friend. He tells the girl this. It is like a request.

"Of course, you'll see him again. Be ready tomorrow. We'll be coming to collect you."

Monsieur Linh's head is spinning. All this is too quick for him, the doctor, the moving.

"At least you're not going to separate us?" It came out like a cry. He clasps his little girl to him. He is ready to fight, to scratch, to bite, to give his last drop of strength.

"The very idea of it, Uncle! Of course not! You'll always be together, both of you, don't worry."

Monsieur Linh calms down. He sits down on the edge of the mattress. He doesn't say anything else. The two women stay on a little while longer, and then the girl reminds him:

"Tomorrow morning, don't forget, be ready!"

Then they go away.

The old man doesn't sleep well. He can feel the little girl lying peacefully beside him, but this doesn't soothe him. It's a night that reminds him of the last night he spent in his homeland, in fear and in the darkness.

He had walked for many days. He had left his village which was no more than ashes. He had gone towards the sea, with *Sang diû* in his arms, and when he finally got there he realised that most of the peasants from other parts of the country, those who had survived, had left as he had done and found themselves there, disoriented, empty-handed, and possessing almost nothing apart from the clothes they were wearing. At the time Monsieur Linh had felt much wealthier than the majority of them. He had his little girl, his own flesh and blood. And he had his tattered suitcase too, containing a few possessions, the old photograph, the cloth bag containing a little soil, the soil of his village, black and full of silt, which he had tilled all his life, as his father had done before him, and his grandfather before that, soil that had fed them and received them when they died.

They had been herded together into a shack made of wooden planks. There were hundreds of them, all crammed together, in silence, not daring to make any noise, not saying a word to one another. Some of them had muttered that they were going to be slaughtered, that the ship would not arrive, that the ferrymen to whom they had given their last coins would cut the throats of every one of them, or else would leave them there for ever.

Monsieur Linh had clasped *Sang diû* to him throughout the night. All around him there was nothing but fear and anxiety, murmurings, rapid breathing and nightmares. Then the white light of morning had dawned. And, towards evening, they spotted the ship, a dilapidated ship, which then drifted for days over the sea beneath the fearsome heat of the sun that beat down upon the hull and the bridge before dropping down into the water, like an extinguished star, as evening fell.

Monsieur Linh can hear the two men who are playing cards at the far end of the dormitory as they tell each other stories in a low voice. They are stories about riches and fabulous fortunes, about jars filled to the brim with piastres somewhere, over there in the homeland. They dream aloud as they slam down their cards. The old man thinks about what they are saying. He thinks about what his homeland really is and about what riches really are. He clasps his little girl even closer. He falls asleep.

The following morning, Monsieur Linh has done his packing.

He has packed his suitcase, as well as the clothing he had been given. He waits. He is ready. The child is also ready, dressed in her simple clothes, the cotton blouse with a pullover on top, some tights and a little pair of trousers provided by the Refugee Bureau. The dress that Monsieur Bark had given her is carefully folded and placed in the suitcase, next to the photograph and the cloth bag containing the handful of soil.

At about ten o'clock, the woman from the quayside and the girl arrive. They greet him.

"We've come to collect you, Uncle," says the girl. He stands up. He feels heavy. The dormitory was not really a very welcoming place, but he had eventually come to feel at ease there. Without fully realising it, he had made it into the surviving part of a destroyed home.

Monsieur Linh says goodbye to the three women who are watching him depart, and to the men who are bent over their cards. The women laugh mischievously and say: "There now, goodbye Uncle, look after yourself! Take good care of the little one especially. Children are delicate creatures!" As for the men, they hold up a hand and wave, without looking at him. That's all.

In the car, the old man does not feel very reassured. He sees streets rushing by that he does not recognise. The rain has started to pour down violently. It streams over the car windows. The city seems diluted behind this moving screen that elongates shapes and blurs the colours as it drowns them.

The journey goes on for a long time. The old man would never have thought the city was so big. It is endless. The two women exchange the occasional word, and then they fall silent. The interpreter girl smiles at him, as if to comfort him. As for the driver, he says nothing. He glides his car into the stream of the traffic.

At last, they arrive. The car draws up outside a large wrought-iron entrance gate. The driver sounds his horn. A man appears through a small door. The driver lowers his window and says a few words to him. The man goes back inside and a few seconds later, the large gate opens, as if by magic. The car follows a long gravel driveway that twists around a park. At the end of this park, at the top of a hill, there is a Mansion. It has stopped raining. When he gets out of the car, Monsieur Linh looks up. The towers of the Mansion are huge. You have the impression that they are lost in the sky. It is a regal abode.

"This is your new home, Uncle," the girl says to him, while he is unable to take his eyes off the towers that soar above his head.

"Here?" asks the old man in disbelief.

"Yes, you'll be fine. Look, there's a lovely park, which is enormous, where you can go for walks. And on the other side, you can glimpse the sea below. "It's wonderful, you wait."

"The sea . . ." Monsieur Linh repeats, without it really sinking in.

The woman from the quayside has taken him by the arm and is leading him inside. The entrance hall is vast. A man comes up to meet them and the woman gives him explanations as she points to Monsieur Linh. In one corner, there is a palm tree in a pot. In another corner, there are three old men wearing dressing gowns made of a thick, blue material. They are sitting in armchairs and they gaze at Monsieur Linh. Their eyes seem dead. Everything about them seems dead.

Monsieur Linh clasps his little girl to him. He thinks of the fat man, his friend, and he thinks to himself that he would love it so much if he were suddenly to appear, now, right here. How happy he would be! But no-one appears apart from a woman dressed in a white coat. The man says a few words to her. She nods, then she addresses the woman from the quayside and the girl.

"Come along, Uncle, we'll show you to your bedroom."

The woman in white wants to carry the old man's suitcase, but he grips the handle and shakes his head. She doesn't insist. She starts walking and invites them to follow her. They go past various corridors and staircases. Occasionally, they come across very elderly men and women, all wearing the same blue dressing gowns, who move about slowly, in silence. All of them stare at Monsieur Linh with a dreary expression. Some of them need the help of walking sticks or crutches, or a strange device that they push in front of them and lean upon.

"There you are, Uncle, this will be your bedroom from now on."

They have just walked into a room with beige walls. Fairly large, bright, and clean. There is a bed, a chair, a small table, an armchair, a bathroom. The woman in white draws the curtain. You can see a tall tree, the top of which is swaying in the wind.

"It's a lovely view, come and see, Uncle."

Monsieur Linh goes over to the window. Trees, the park and its lawns that are as green as the leaves of a banana tree, and in the distance the rooftops of the city, a vast number of them, clustered together; the city dotted over the hills, with its streets, its crowds, its cars that criss-cross it in every direction, its roar of motors, of horns hooting, and somewhere, down there, he doesn't know where, in the midst of this vast space, the fat man, his friend, who has not seen him for two days and who must be wondering what has happened.

"We shall come to see you regularly. You'll see, the people are very kind here, they'll look after you, and you won't lack for anything."

The girl smiles.

"And my cigarettes?" asks Monsieur Linh.

The girl speaks to the woman from the quayside, and then to the woman in white. All three of them exchange a few words.

"It's forbidden to smoke here, Uncle. And smoking, you know, is very bad for your health."

Monsieur Linh suddenly feels sad, as if his body had just been cut open to remove an organ that is useless and yet at the same time essential. Yes, there is a hollow inside him. He is filled with a great weariness, but he doesn't want the child to be aware of this. He has to be strong, for the child. *Sang diû* needs him. She is still so small, and so frail. He is not allowed to be weak, or to complain about his lot.

"Everything will be alright," he says to the girl.

A little later, when he is alone again with the child, in the bedroom, and the girl, the woman from the quayside and the woman in white have all left, Monsieur Linh looks at the bare, beige walls. Then he remembers the large cages that he noticed in the Park, which the families and children were hurrying along to look at. And then, like an invisible arrow fired at his heart, in his mind's eye he sees the immensity of the rice fields that flank the mountainside and that stretch out their green plumes as far as the sea, which they knew was over there, far away, without any of them ever going to see it.

He sits down on the bed, takes the child on his lap, strokes her forehead and her cheeks, and runs his thin, gnarled fingers over her little mouth and her eyelids. He closes his eyes and hums the song.

When dusk falls, the woman in white comes back to see him. She brings him some pyjamas as well as a blue dressing gown. She explains to him that he must wear these clothes. She waits, with her arms folded. Monsieur Linh lays his little girl on the bed and goes into the bathroom. He puts on the pyjamas, and slips on the dressing gown. It is too big for him. It almost touches the ground. It is a strange outfit. When he comes back into the bedroom, the woman in white looks at him and smiles, but it is not an unpleasant smile, more an amused, affectionate smile. She takes in her arms the old clothes that Monsieur Linh was wearing and she goes away.

The old man feels very odd. There is a full-length mirror behind his bedroom door. He looks at himself in it, and he sees a puppet dressed in a long blue garment. The puppet looks as if he is lost in his clothing, and his hands disappear up his sleeves. His expression is infinitely sad.

Night falls. Seated on his bed, Monsieur Linh has taken his child in his arms. He is cradling her. The woman in white comes back and explains to him that he must follow her. She walks quickly. The old man scurries after her, hampered by the folds of his dressing gown which keep flapping open and shut. They go past various corridors and staircases and arrive at last in a large hall. There are about thirty tables there, and around these tables, busy drinking their soup, are groups of ten or more men and women who are all elderly and are dressed identically in the same blue dressing gowns.

The woman in white leads Monsieur Linh to an empty chair. He sits down between two men. Two other men and a woman sitting between them are opposite him. No-one looks up as he takes his seat. He is brought a bowl of soup. *Sang diû* is on his lap. He ties the napkin round her neck, but the child is like him and does not seem very hungry: the soup runs down her lips and onto her chin. Monsieur Linh wipes her, starts again, and so as to set a good example to the little girl, he drinks a few spoonfuls himself.

The other guests pay no attention to him. They do not look at anything. Some have their heads drooped over their plates. Others are gazing vacantly at a very distant point in the hall. Some of their faces are prone to a constant shaking and are smeared with soup. Nobody talks. It is a strange silence. All that can be heard is the sound of spoons on bowls, mouths slurping, and occasional sneezes. Nothing else.

Monsieur Linh thinks of the dormitory again, of the jeering women, their gambling husbands, their noisy children. He is surprised that he misses them, that he misses those families who spoke his language even though they scarcely ever addressed him. But at least he was still living amid the music of the words of his homeland, in their beautiful, high-pitched, nasal lament. All that is a long time ago. Why does he have to distance himself from so many things? Why should the end of his life consist of nothing but disappearance, death and burial?

Monsieur Linh hugs the child tightly to him. The meal is over. The old people are already getting to their feet, accompanied by a scraping of chairs, and departing, followed by others. The hall is empty. Monsieur Linh has not the strength to stand up. It is the woman in white who comes to collect him and take him back to his bedroom. She murmurs a few words, and goes away.

The old man walks to the window. The wind is no longer shaking the tall tree, but the night has brought out thousands of lights in the city that sparkle and seem to move about. It is as if they were stars that had fallen to earth and were trying to fly back into the sky once more. But they are unable to do so. You can never fly back to what you have lost, Monsieur Linh reflects.

The days go by. The old man has got to know his new home, the difficult route past the corridors and staircases, the location of the dining hall, and that of the armchair room as he calls it, for there are armchairs almost everywhere in this room; armchairs that await you. He has also learnt to know the times at which he has to make his way to the dining hall. He sits always in the same place there, at the same table, beside the same silent old men. He has got used to the blue dressing gown, even finding the too-voluminous material useful since it enables him to wrap it around his little girl when he takes her for walks in the Mansion and the weather grows a little chilly.

What does surprise him about this new place is that the people around him, those who are dressed like him, are all indifferent to one another, like the pedestrians on the city pavements. No-one looks at anyone else. No-one speaks to anyone. Only occasionally does a quarrel break out and two residents begin to squabble, he does not really know why, but very quickly a woman in white appears and separates them.

Monsieur Linh does everything he can to avoid an old woman who had pursued him in the park. She had come up to him initially when he was not watching, and then she had grabbed hold of the child and tried to pick her up. She had held on to her tightly, laughing as she did so, but Monsieur Linh had succeeded in pushing the old woman away, who then began to run after him along the pathways, shouting as she went. He had hidden behind a bush, whispering in the child's ear to comfort her. The old woman had not seen them and had gone on her way. Ever since, whenever he catches sight of this crazy creature in the distance, he does an about-turn.

The park is big. The weather is increasingly mild. During the daytime, Monsieur Linh is often outside in the sunshine. Sometimes he takes off his blue dressing gown so that he is clad only in his pyjamas – the day-time pyjamas, for it has been made clear to him that there is one pair for the day-time and another for the night-time – but a woman in white quickly arrives and asks him to put it back on. So he puts it back on, without complaining.

When he gazes over the city, Monsieur Linh never stops thinking of the fat man, his friend. And when he looks at the sea, he never stops thinking of his lost homeland. And thus the view of the sea and that of the city make him sad in the same way. Time passes and carves out a painful hollow inside him. There is the little girl, of course, and he must be strong for her, put on a good face, and sing her the song as if there were nothing wrong. He must be cheerful for her sake, he must smile at her and feed her, see that she sleeps well, that she grows up and becomes a beautiful little girl. But time has taken its toll, it wounds the old man's soul, gnaws at his heart and cuts short his breath.

He would so like to see his friend again. He would so like to ask the interpreter girl what he should do to see him again, but the interpreter girl does not come back any more and nor does the woman from the quayside. That is why, after thinking carefully about it, Monsieur Linh decides to manage on his own, to go into the city by himself, to find the street where the dormitory is, and the one where the bench and the park are, and to sit on the bench and wait patiently, for as long as necessary, to see his friend, the fat man, at last.

He waits for the right day, a very fine day. And that day comes. Monsieur Linh has everything planned. He will set off after the midday meal. Being among the first to arrive in the dining hall, he eats a good helping, finishing everything on his plate and taking twice as much food, for he will need his strength. A woman in white comes over, puts her hand on his shoulder, and smiles as she watches him eat. His table companions still show no interest. The pupils of their eyes are like glass pebbles lying in the midst of a puddle of water, the rims of which are slightly red. Monsieur

Linh is unconcerned. He eats, and he eats so much that eventually he feels heavy, heavy and strong. He can set off. Yes, now he can set off.

Sang diû has fallen asleep on his shoulder. He has left the dining hall and he is walking at a good pace down the central driveway of the park, the one he was driven along by car on the first day. As he gets further away from the Mansion, he no longer comes across any other residents, but only the birds that spring out from the bushes, pull large, wriggling worms out of the grass, and hop about on the gravel, chirping now and then.

Monsieur Linh notices the large iron entrance gate, and just beside him, a small hut. The gate is closed, but about three yards away, there is a narrow door that opens in the wall. The old man makes his way towards it. And it is at the moment that he grabs hold of the handle and starts to push open the door that he hears someone yelling behind him. As he turns round, he sees a man coming out of the hut and walking swiftly towards him. The man is speaking to him, but Monsieur Linh has the impression that he is barking. He recognises him: it is the man who had opened the two gates on the day of his arrival, after exchanging a few words with the taxi driver.

The old man is not disconcerted and continues to push open the door. He can already see the roadway, but the man who is barking is now close behind him and, with a violent thrust of his hand, he shuts the door again, stands in front of it and pushes Monsieur Linh away.

"I want to go out," the old man says, "I have a friend I must meet."

The other man does not understand a word, of course. He does not speak his language, but Monsieur Linh continues speaking to him all the same, telling him that he wants to go out, that he has something he has to do, and that he must be allowed through.

The man simply holds him at a distance by reaching out his hand and keeping it on Monsieur Linh's scrawny chest. As he does this, he speaks to a device that he holds in his other hand and which crackles from time to time. Soon, hurried footsteps can be heard, pacing along the driveway from the Mansion. There are two women in white, followed by a man, also in white.

"I want to get out," Monsieur Linh says again. They surround him. The two women try to calm him down and lead him away, but he does not allow them to do so. With his free hand, he hangs onto the door handle and with his other hand he clasps his little girl by the waist so that she does not fall.

The smiles and the gentleness slowly fade from the faces of the two women in white. The man in white then comes up and loosens Monsieur Linh's fingers one by one from the door handle. He is now held firmly, but he struggles with all his might. One of the women brings out a rectangular-shaped metal box from her overall pocket. She opens it and takes out a syringe, on which she checks the level by squirting a few drops of a substance from the needle. She lifts up the left sleeve of Monsieur Linh's dressing gown, then his pyjama sleeve, and injects the muscle of his arm.

Gradually, the old man stops struggling and talking. He can feel his body weakening and growing warm. The trees swirl above his head. The faces of the people who surround him are becoming misshapen and elongated. Their voices take on a muffled echo and the gravel path is transformed into a watery snake whose scales gleam beneath the blue sky. Before passing out completely, he just has time to see one of the women, not the one who gave the injection but the other one, pick up *Sang diû* and take her in her arms. Then, Monsieur Linh, relieved to know that the child has not fallen to the ground, allows himself to glide down the steep slope of artificial sleep.

It is a night that never ends. A night such as he has never known before. It seems to last for a hundred years, but its blackness is not in the least disconcerting. To begin with, the old man has the feeling of being inside one of those caves that pit the mountainside overlooking his village and which are the haunts of bats. Monsieur Linh is walking through the cave towards a distant point, one of incandescent brilliance and whiteness. As he walks, he can feel his strength returning to his body. His muscles ripple smoothly beneath his skin. His legs are sturdy and carry him wonderfully well. When he reaches the entrance to the cave, the daylight dazzles him. The sun shines through the leaves of the tall trees that are buzzing with the cries of monkeys and birds calling. The old man blinks. All this light that streams through his blindness, while at the same time filling him with a deep, ineffable joy. The joy of a child.

Once his eyes have grown accustomed to the light, he notices the presence of a man, sitting on a rock, a few yards away. The man has his back to him. He is gazing at the forest scenery. He is smoking a cigarette. Dead branches crackle beneath Monsieur Linh's feet. The man turns around and notices him. He smiles and shakes his head with pleasure. Monsieur Linh smiles too when he realises that the man who is sitting down is his friend, the fat man.

"You've been a long time! I've smoked ten cigarettes already. I was wondering whether you were going to come . . ." said the fat man, pretending to be angry.

Monsieur Linh understands perfectly what his friend is saying and is not even surprised by the fact.

"It's just that it's a long way. I walked and walked, it never seemed to end," he replied.

The fat man also appears to understand perfectly what Monsieur Linh is saying and does not seem surprised either.

"I was frightened that you would have already left, that you wouldn't have waited for me . . ."

"You must be joking," the fat man said. "I'm always so happy each time I see you. I would have waited for days and days if need be."

The words just spoken touched the old man deeply. He gave his friend a hug, and simply said to him: "Come".

The two friends set off. They walk down the path that wends its way through the forest. It is a day of incomparable beauty. The air is fragrant with the smell of damp earth and frangipani blossom. The moss looks like cushions embroidered with jade and the bamboo trees quiver with the rustle of a thousand birds. Monsieur Linh leads the way. He often turns round to his friend and, by word or by sign, points to a root that might cause him to trip, or else a branch that might injure him.

The forest gives way to the plain. The two men stop on the outskirts of the forest and they gaze across the green expanse which in the far distance opens out towards the shimmering blue of the sea.

In the rice fields, the women plant the young rice shoots, singing as they do so. Their feet disappear into the warm, muddy water. The buffalos are lost in contemplation, heads lowered, while oxpeckers parade up and down their backs, preening their white feathers. The children are trying to catch frogs, yelling and striking the water with willow sticks. In the sky, swallows are writing invisible poems in the light breeze.

"How beautiful it is!" the fat man exclaims.

"It's my homeland . . ." Monsieur Linh says, waving his arm as if he were the lord of the manor.

Both of them continue their walk along a wide path. Occasionally, they come across peasants on their way home from the markets, their yokes considerably lighter. Business had been good. Monsieur Linh greets them and introduces his friend. They exchange a word or two. They go on their way wishing one another much happiness.

When they arrive within sight of Monsieur Linh's village, they are already being followed by a whole troop of children whom the old man shouts at and reprimands. But there is nothing malicious in his words because these screeching children, this gang of brown-skinned, dark-eyed kids, with their ink-black hair that is impervious to the sun, with their rounded bellies, their milky smiles and their bare feet, they are the new shoots, the dawn of the future, the tide of vigour that streams through his village, his homeland, the place he loves and carries in the deepest core of his being.

"Here is the house of *brother* Duk. And here is the house of *brother* Lanh. This is the house of *brother* Nang. Over there, that's *brother* Thiep's, here . . ."

Monsieur Linh introduces his friend to all the houses in the village. He introduces him to the elder members of his own family too, should they be sitting beside their doors, warming their old bones in the sunshine. They greet one another by bowing their heads and placing their hands together. The fat man smiles. He tells Monsieur Linh that he has not felt so happy for a long time.

Pigs are rolling around in the dusty hollows of the main street. Dogs are scratching themselves or yawning as they lie stretched out. Hens are squabbling over stray specks of grain. In the shade of an immense banyan tree that is several hundred years old, some old women are weaving bamboo mats. Beside them, three toddlers are sitting on their bottoms and are playing with a feather stuck into a cork.

"And here is my house." Monsieur Linh smiles at his friend. He points to his home and invites him to go in. The fat man starts to climb the ladder, which bends beneath his weight.

"Are you sure it will hold?" he says.

"I made it myself," Monsieur Linh says. "An elephant could go up it, don't worry!"

Both of them laugh.

Once they have reached the house's one room, Monsieur Linh invites his friend to sit down. A meal awaits them. Monsieur Linh's daughter-in-law has prepared it, before setting out for the fields, with his son and their child, little *Sang diû*.

The dishes are arranged on plates and in bowls. There is water-spinach and lemongrass soup, prawns sautéed in garlic, a stuffed crab, vegetable noodles, some pork in sweet-and-sour sauce, banana fritters and sticky rice cakes. It is a real feast. The delicious aromas of the various foods waft through the house: fresh corian-der, cinnamon, ginger, vegetables and caramel. Monsieur Linh encourages his friend to try these dishes and he helps himself generously, filling his plate several times from each bowl. He has not taken such pleasure in eating for ages. He pours small glasses of rice beer. They both drink and eat, and smile at one another. Through the windows of the room, one can see the rice fields and the sunlight sparkling on the water.

"I've never eaten anything so good," the fat man says. "Please congratulate the cook."

"She really is a good cook," Monsieur Linh says. "What's more, my son loves her and she loves my son. And she has given him a beautiful child."

The old man places both hands on his stomach. There is nothing left in the bowls or on the plates. The two friends have eaten their fill.

"Please, do smoke," Monsieur Linh says to the fat man. "I like the smell of your cigarettes."

Whereupon the fat man takes a pack from his pocket, taps the bottom with his yellowish fingers, and offers it to Monsieur Linh, who shakes his head and smiles. The fat man takes a cigarette, slips it between his lips, lights it, inhales the first puff and closes his eyes.

The day wears on. The heat in the open house is like a sweeping caress that soothes the body. The two friends admire the landscape, look at one another and exchange a few words. The hours go by. Monsieur Linh points to the mountains that stand guard around them like the rims of a crater, and their crests seem to quiver a little and vanish into the sky. He names each mountain, and he recounts the legend that is attached to every one of them. Some of the stories are terrifying. Others, on the other hand, are light-hearted and amusing. The fat man listens attentively to him while smoking his countless cigarettes.

Before the evening begins to cast its musky imprint over the ground, Monsieur Linh says to the fat man:

"Come along now, it's getting chilly again. We can go for a walk. I want to take you to see something."

Here they are once more in the village street, then later among the rice fields, then in the forest. The scraping sound of the locusts' wings, the cries of the monkeys and the songs of the birds go before them, envelop them and pursue them. Monsieur Linh walks ahead, in his hand a bamboo cane which he uses to beat back the prickly grasses that sometimes bow down over the path, and he sings; he is singing the song:

> *Always there is the morning*
> *Always the light returns*
> *Always there is another day*
> *One day it's you who will be a mother.*

"It's a beautiful song," says the fat man. "I've always loved hearing you sing it."

"Normally it's the women who hum it, but I know the little girl likes it when I sing it to her, which is why I whisper it to her very often, close to her ear, and I can see her eyes light up. Even in her sleep, I know that her eyes are gleaming. But listen carefully,"

Monsieur Linh says. "Here is another song."

And he puts his hand to his ear so as to ask his friend to pay attention.

A sound of trickling water seems to be coming from the forest even though there is no sign of any river or any stream in this area. Yet it is nevertheless the sound of water that can be heard, the sound of running water.

Monsieur Linh beckons to his friend to follow him. He leaves the path and plunges into the forest. The last of the sunshine is casting patches of gold here and there over the carpet of moss, and suddenly, bursting out of this green mosaic mingled with flame, a spring appears. It arises from between two stones and the water that gushes forth follows five paths, as if it were charting the shape of an outstretched hand and outspread fingers and thumb: an open hand, a proffered hand. The five streams of water then disappear into the ground a few feet away as miraculously as they had risen up to the daylight.

"This spring is no ordinary spring," Monsieur Linh says to the fat man. "It is said that its waters have the power to heal the person who drinks them, to heal the memory of unpleasant things. When one of us knows he is going to die, he sets off to the spring, on his own. The whole village knows where he is going, but no-one goes with him. He must make his own way there, and be on his own when he kneels down here. He comes to drink the water from the spring, and as soon as he has drunk it, his memory becomes hazy: all that it retains are the joyful moments and the good times, everything that is pleasant and happy. The other memories, those that cut, those that wound, those that pierce the soul and devour it, they all disappear, diluted in the water like a drop of ink in the ocean."

Monsieur Linh stops speaking. The fat man nods. It is as if he were rolling around in his mind all the words he has just heard.

"There," Monsieur Linh continues, "now you know where we shall have to go when we feel death drawing near."

"We still have time!" his friend replies with a laugh.

"Yes," Monsieur Linh says. He is laughing himself. "You are right, we do indeed have time ..."

The weather is so fine. The evening mingles with all the smells of the earth.

And, since it is beginning to get late, the two friends return by the path to the cave. The fat man smokes a last cigarette as he walks and its menthol aroma blends with those of the ferns and the bark. Once they reach the entrance to the cave, the two friends stop. The fat man surveys the landscape once more.

"What a lovely day we have spent!"

Monsieur Linh smiles at his friend and clasps him in his arms.

"Don't be late. See you soon."

"Yes, see you soon. And thanks again, truly. Thank you."

The fat man goes into the cave. Monsieur Linh gazes after him. He watches his silhouette being slowly swallowed up by the darkness, a hand waving him goodbye, and afterwards nothing more.

Then the old man closes his eyes.

When he awakes, Monsieur Linh feels as if he is chained up. But no, he is mistaken, there is nothing restraining him, his wrists are free, and so are his ankles. He is in his bedroom. Where is *Sang diû*? He sits bolt upright. His heart skips a beat, stops, and starts again. The little girl is there, lying on the armchair. He gets to his feet, takes her in his arms, brings her back into bed with him and holds her very tight.

His memory comes back to him. He sees himself walking towards the large entrance gate. He can see the face of the man who spoke in a loud voice. He can see the women and the man in white. He remembers the injection, and his falling asleep.

The old man has a very bad headache and he is thirsty. A consuming thirst. But it is not just his thirst that consumes him. There is a question as well: where is he? What is this place in which he finds himself and which he is forbidden to leave? Is it a hospital? But he is not ill! Is it a prison? Yet he has done nothing wrong. And then, how long has it been since the injection? Was it the same day? The day after? The following month?

Who looked after *Sang diû*? Had she been fed properly, washed, stroked?

The little girl does not appear to be anxious or upset. She is sleeping peacefully. Monsieur Linh keeps his eyes wide open. He is thinking of his friend, the fat man. He thinks of him with sadness and hope. He can see his smile. He tells himself that no entrance gate is going to prevent him from finding him, nor a man who barks, nor any of the dozens of women in white, or any injections. He tells himself this, and suddenly he feels strong again, invulnerable and at the same time light-headed, whereas a moment ago his exhaustion knew no bounds.

The following morning, Monsieur Linh takes his place among the inmates once more. Wearing his blue dressing gown, he walks slowly down the corridors, goes calmly into the dining hall, finds his table, and shows no sign of hurry, anxiety, ravenous hunger or despondency. He is well aware that the women in white are paying particular attention to him and are watching him out of the corners of their eyes. The old man keeps close to the walls, returns the smiles, lowers his gaze, and takes walks in the park without ever going beyond the unwritten limits. Sometimes, he sits down on a bench, cradles his little girl, talks to her, whispers sweet nothings in her ears and gazes at the sea below, in the distance, with its ruffled waves and its currents. In the evening, after dinner, he is the first to return to his bedroom, go to bed, and switch off his light after the woman in white who is on night duty has made her last round.

Monsieur Linh conforms to this regimen for several days. Everything returns to normal. He is no longer observed. He is merely an old man. A frail and slender shadow among the hundreds of frail and slender shadows dressed in blue flannel who noiselessly come and go along the pathways of the large park.

Sang diû does not appear to mind the new situation. She is an unselfish child. The old man tells himself that his little girl does everything she can not to annoy him. She is only a few months old, but she already knows so many things. Very soon she will be a young girl, then a teenager, then a young lady. Time goes rapidly by. Life goes rapidly by, transforming the young lotus buds into the large flowers that are spread over the perimeter of the lakes.

Monsieur Linh would like to see his child blossom. He wants to live in order to see this, and what does it matter what life has in store, whether it be far from his homeland that he has to live, or here, in this house with its restraining walls. No, he does not want it to be here. Not in this place where people are left to die. He wants *Sang diû* to become the most beautiful of the lotus flowers, and he wants to be there to admire her, but he wants to admire her in the daylight, in the open air, not in a home, not in a prison like this one. His friend will be able to help him. Only he will really be able to help him. He will explain to him, with gestures. He will understand, for sure. He wants to see the fat man – his friend, whom he misses so – again. He wants to hear his voice, his laugh. He wants to smell the aroma of the cigarettes that he is forever smoking. He wants to look at his large hands, damaged by hard work. He wants to feel his presence, his warmth and his strength.

It is the third day of spring. It is early. Monsieur Linh is the first to leave the dining room after having had his breakfast. The other residents are still there, dipping their bread into their tea or their coffee, as he steps briskly across the lawns. He knows that at this early hour the men and women in white are all in a small room, next door to the dining room. They, too, are drinking tea or coffee, and are chatting and joking. It is the time of day when supervision is at its most lax.

Monsieur Linh does not make for the entrance gate. He makes for a copse he had seen from his bedroom window. He knows that behind this copse the outer wall of the park is not as high as it is elsewhere and that the branch of a tree almost touches it.

He walks at speed, clutching his little girl to his ribs; sometimes she opens her eyes as if to ask him what he is doing. Here we are; he goes up to the wall. He was quite right. The wall is not very high. It is the height of his head. The whole of the upper part has collapsed. What should he do? The branch he had seen from his window is of no use. It is too high up. Monsieur Linh then discovers, lying on the ground, a dead tree trunk covered in protruding spurs. He lays *Sang diû* on the ground, drags the tree trunk along and props it against the wall. He should be able to use it as a ladder. He tries it out. Yes, it is fine, it reaches the top of the wall easily. But how will he get down again on the other side? With the child?

Then Monsieur Linh thinks of the women in his village, and of the way they carry their new-born babies when they set off to work in the rice fields or collect dead wood in the forest. He takes off his dressing gown, places the infant inside it, having made sure that the old photograph as well as the little bag containing the earth from his homeland do not fall out of the pocket into which he had put them. Then he ties the dressing gown tightly to his back. The little girl is thus pressed in closely behind her grandfather. She cannot fall out. The old man climbs up the makeshift ladder. Once he has reached the top of the wall, he hauls up the dead tree trunk, gathers his breath, casts his eye over the park, and observes that nothing is moving and that nobody is watching him. He tips the tree trunk over to the other side. He climbs down in a hurry and sets foot on the pavement of a deserted road. He is free. This has taken only a few minutes. He is free and he is wearing his pyjamas, with a child tied to his back with a knotted dressing gown. He is happy. It would not take much for him to shout aloud with joy. With small, rapid steps he leaves the Mansion behind. It is as if he were twenty years old.

Monsieur Linh walks quickly down towards the town. He has put on his dressing gown once more and is carrying his little girl in his arms. The streets of the neighbourhood he is passing through are deserted. Now and then, he comes across a man walking his dog, or municipal workers busy sweeping the gutters. But they neither look up nor take any notice of him.

When he feels far enough away from the Mansion, the old man stops to sit down on a bench, to rest a little and, in particular, to dress *Sang diû* in the beautiful costume the fat man had given her, which he had made sure he took away with him, neatly folded. She looks wonderful. Monsieur Linh feels proud to be the grand-father of such a child.

From his bedroom window, the old man had had time to observe the city, to try to understand it, to discover the layout of its thoroughfares, the location of the area where the dormitory building was, the café he used to go to with the fat man, the bench where they met. And so, as he walks, he has convinced himself that he is going in the right direction and that he will very soon rediscover all those places that had become familiar to him.

Monsieur Linh thinks of the expression that will be on his friend's face when he sees him again, for he does not doubt for a second that they will meet one another. The city is large, certainly, it is vast even, but it will not prevent this reunion that makes the old man smile when he thinks of it.

Gradually, the delightful houses with their gardens disappear. The broad avenues are now lined with factories painted in dreary metallic colours. Lorries are waiting in front of the depots. Beside the lorries, there are men chatting as they bide their time. Some of them see Monsieur Linh pass by. They whistle at him. They seem to be speaking to him in their loud voices, and laughing. The old man nods to them and hurries on.

These avenues are never-ending. You cannot see where they finish. And there are always these lines of buildings carrying out unlikely functions, into which the lorries drive, and out of which the lorries emerge in a deafening choreography embellished by exhaust fumes and prolonged sounding of horns. It all gives Monsieur Linh a headache. He is worried that his little girl may be frightened so he blocks her ears with his hands. But the child, true to her docile nature, says nothing. Her eyes open and close. She is calm. Nothing disturbs her.

The old man's legs and feet are starting to hurt. It is not easy to walk in slippers. And the dressing gown is too warm now because the sun, climbing ever higher in the sky, is beginning to beat down fiercely. For the first time, Monsieur Linh experiences a dent in his confidence, a doubt: supposing he were not on the right road? Supposing he were lost? He stops and looks about him. This does not tell him very much. In the distance, he notices nothing in particular other than the white birds that rise up from the roofs of the tall windowless buildings and the tops of the revolving cranes, wheeling in tightly bunched flocks over these steel crests.

Seeing this, the old man remembers the dismal day of his arrival in this land, in this city. He shivers, in spite of the heat. Suddenly, it is as if he could once again feel on his skin the icy fine rain of that afternoon that is at once recent and long ago. It is the cranes that have reminded him of this. The cranes at the port. He thinks, he stops. If the big port is down there, it means that the little fishing port is likely to be around here, and if it is around here, then the bench where they met can only be in this direction.

Monsieur Linh veers off to the left. He feels encouraged again. He even feels amused, thinking of the men and women in white who are looking for him, over there at the Mansion, and who must be searching every nook and cranny of the building, and all the hidden places in the park. What must the expressions on their faces be like!

Suddenly, just as he was laughing, he failed to see the hole in the road, filled with greasy water. His left foot sinks into it. He loses his balance, almost falls, and just manages to readjust himself by hopping. His foot is naked. The slipper is still in the hole, caught on the jagged grate of a manhole. As he clasps the little girl to him, he tries to recover his slipper. It is stuck deep in the bottom of the hole. He pulls. It gives way. He finds himself holding a torn slipper in his hand, drenched in foul-smelling water. Unusable. The old man is desolate. He tries as best he can to wring the slipper dry and he puts it on again: half of his foot protrudes through it. He sets off again. His pace grows slower. He drags one leg as if he were limping. A disgusting smell accompanies him. He had not paid attention to the sleeve of his dressing gown or the two hems of his garment that had become soaked in the foul water when he had tried to get his slipper back. All of a sudden, the sun seems less of an ally, and he feels increasingly weighed down by weariness. *Sang diû* does not appear to have noticed anything. She is asleep, happy and unconcerned by all these minor incidents.

Monsieur Linh is no longer the only person on the pavement. It is not yet as bad as the crowds that rush along the street where the bench where they meet is, but he encounters more and more men and women, and children who are holding one another by the hand and running and rushing about. He also notices that he has left the factory area behind.

All around him now are buildings that are not very tall, usually with a shop – a grocery store, a launderette, a fishmonger – or a business on the ground floor. Young people are chatting among themselves on the street corners. Police cars flash by, all sirens blaring. People stare at him, not in a hostile way, but more in astonishment. The old man senses that some of them are making comments to one another about him as they see him pass by. He thinks to himself that he probably does not cut much of a figure, what with his torn gown and his useless slipper. He puts his head down and tries to walk faster.

He roams around this area for more than three hours, believing that he is making headway, not realising that he keeps coming back to the same roundabout that he has walked past four times already. The noises, the music that comes from the open windows of the apartments or the enormous radio sets that some teenagers carry on their shoulders, the car exhaust, the roaring of the engines, the smells of cooking and of rotten fruit thrown on the pavements, all these things make him reel and weigh him down even more.

He is walking slowly now. Because he is limping and dragging his leg, he has a shooting pain in his hip. The child in his arms weighs a ton. Monsieur Linh is thirsty. He is hungry too. He stops for a moment, leans against a lamppost, and pulls out of his pocket a small plastic bag into which he had put a bit of brioche dipped in milk and water. He tries to feed *Sang diû*, without staining her beautiful dress. He eats two mouthfuls himself.

But all of a sudden a woman comes out of the florist's shop close to where he had stopped. She comes straight up to him. She must be the owner. She is holding a broom in her hand, which she waves above her head. She is shouting. She points with her broom at Monsieur Linh. She calls the other people as her witness, shows them his bare foot in the torn slipper and the foul-smelling stains on his sleeves. She indicates to the old man that he should go away, clear off. She points to the end of the road, to the far distance. A crowd has gathered. Monsieur Linh is rigid with shame. The woman does not stop, encouraged as she is by the shouts of the onlookers. She struts about. She looks like some kind of large guinea-fowl in a rage, angrily scratching about in the farmyard dung-heap. The old man puts the plastic bag in his pocket straightaway and flees. The people laugh as they watch him depart, dragging his leg like a wounded animal. The fat woman yells out a few more words that she hurls at him like pebbles. As for the laughs, they are knives, sharpened knives that find his heart and cleave it.

Monsieur Linh no longer sees the sun, no longer feels the first, yet ever so delicate warmth of springtime. He advances like a robot, devoting his meagre strength to clasping the child in his arms and placing one foot in front of the other. He no longer takes any notice of either the streets or the houses.

With his wild and staring eyes, he has become a vagabond.

The hours go by, and it is already late in the afternoon. He has been walking since the morning. Since the morning he has been clinging to the hope of finding the street, the bench, and his friend sitting on the bench. His thoughts are becoming muddled. He says to himself that he was probably wrong to leave in the way he did. He tells himself that the city is too big, that it is a monster that will devour him, or lose him. He thinks that he will never ever find anything again, neither his homeland, nor his friend, nor even the Mansion that he set out from. He is cross with himself. Not because he is miserable, weary and crushed. No, he is not thinking of himself. He is cross with himself on his little girl's account. It is he who is inflicting this weariness on her, this bouncing about as he walks, the dust of the streets, the din, the jeering of the passers-by. What sort of grandfather is he? Shame seeps through him like a poison.

He is leaning against a wall. Slowly, without him even being aware of it, he sinks down to the ground. It is like a fall that could last a second or else a lifetime, a slow fall onto the tarmac of the pavement. Down he goes, he is on the ground, his child lying across his knees. Monsieur Linh's head is heavy with too much weariness, suffering and disappointment. It is heavy with too many defeats and too many departures. So what is human life other than a string of wounds that one wears around one's neck? What is the point of going on like this over the days, months and years, ever weaker and more battered? Why should the future always be bleaker than the days that have passed, which were bad enough already?

The thoughts jostle around in his head. Only at the last moment does he notice a man's feet, close to him. He looks up. The man is tall. He speaks to him, he points at Monsieur Linh's bare foot; he points at the little girl. His face is not unkind. He goes on talking. The old man does not understand anything, of course. The man bends down, looks for something in his coat pocket and puts it in Monsieur Linh's right hand, then with a gentle movement he closes the hand, stands up, nods his head and goes on his way.

The old man opens his hand and looks to see what the passer-by has just left in it. There are three coins, three coins that gleam in the sunlight. The man has given alms to him. The man has taken him for a beggar. Monsieur Linh can feel tears dripping down his dry cheeks.

Afterwards, a long time afterwards, he is on his feet again, walking once more. He is not thinking of anything apart from clasping to him as tightly as possible his little girl, who is there, always so well behaved, and beautiful in her pink silk dress. Monsieur Linh presses on. He is a robot who totters along, walks slowly, jostles and is jostled himself by the increasingly rough and dense crowd that surrounds him and stifles him. He no longer sees anything, no longer hears anything. He looks at the ground. It is as if his eyes were leaden weights and were forcing him to gaze at this land that is not his own, that will never be his, and over which he is compelled to make his way, just as a convict is compelled to endure his punishment. For hours on end.

Everything becomes confused. The places, the days, the faces. The old man sees his village once more, the rice fields with their draughtboard formation that can look either dull or sparkling, according to the time of day, the paddy tied in bundles, the ripe mangoes, the eyes of his friend, the fat man, whose thick fingers are stained yellow by tobacco, the features of his son, the crater left by the bomb, the disembowelled corpses, the village in flames. He presses on. He stumbles past the years and past people who are rushing somewhere, who are forever rushing, as if it were a peculiarity of men to rush, to rush towards a large precipice without ever stopping.

All of a sudden, a sharp pain in the shoulder drags him away from the swirling crowd which was drawing him on relentlessly.

A young man carrying a box in his arms had just crashed into him. He is flustered. He speaks to Monsieur Linh and asks him if he is alright. The old man has not let go of the child. He holds her up in his arms. She opens her eyes. She is fine. The young man waits for an answer that does not come, then he goes away.

Monsieur Linh picks himself up and looks around him. There are hordes of people, men, women, children, entire families, who are happily surging between two gates that are wide open. Beyond these gates, large trees can be seen, flower-beds, pathways, and cages. Cages.

The old man can feel his heart racing. Cages. With animals. He can see them. Lions. Monkeys. Bears. Monsieur Linh suddenly has the sense of being inside a picture that he has often gazed at. The Park! He is opposite the entrance to the Park! The Park with the merry-go-round and the wooden horses! But then, if he is there, it means that on the other side, the other side ... Yes, over there, on the far side of the road where hundreds of cars are passing by, there is the bench! And on the bench, like an apparition, a vast apparition that is substantial and all too real, is the fat man, his friend. His friend, who is waiting for him!

Monsieur Linh forgets everything. His great weariness, his bare foot, his dressing gown spattered with filthy water, the deep despair that barely a few seconds ago had overwhelmed him. The sun has never shone so brightly. The sky has never been so clear at the onset of dusk. The old man has not felt such an intense feeling of joy for a very long time.

Trembling, he moves closer to the road, trembling, and he shouts out. He shouts the only words of the native language that he knows. He shouts them out aloud so that his cry should reach beyond the cars and the din they make. "Good-day! Good-day!" Monsieur Linh calls to his friend sitting on the bench, less than a hundred yards away. "Good-day!" he yells, as if his very life depended purely on these simple words.

Monsieur Bark crushes his mentholated cigarette under his heel. He is feeling weary, and useless. He has been coming to this bench for days and days. He spends entire afternoons there, alone, on weekdays, and now even on Sundays. Monsieur Tao-laï has never come back. Monsieur Bark keeps thinking of the old man. He liked him so much. He liked his smile, his thoughtfulness, his respectful silence, the song he hummed, and his gestures too. The old man was his friend. They understood one another; no need for lengthy speeches.

Monsieur Bark had tried to find out what could possibly have happened. After a few days, once he had resigned himself to the fact that Monsieur Tao-Laï would probably not come back to their meeting-place any more, he went to the building which he had accompanied him to so many times. The housekeeper had told him that there had indeed been a dormitory for refugees on the first floor, but that it was now closed. The premises had been sold. In its place there would soon be either an insurance office, or an advertising agency, he was not too sure.

Monsieur Bark described his friend to him.

"Yes," the housekeeper had said, "I know just whom you mean, he was harmless enough, a bit solitary that's all, but harmless enough. I sometimes tried to talk to him, but he didn't understand the slightest word. The others often made fun of him incidentally, but he's no longer there. Some women came to collect him."

At the Refugee Bureau, which he eventually went to next, he was told, after they had checked lengthy lists, that they knew no-one by the name of Tao-laï. He set off again, not knowing what else he could do.

It is getting late. Monsieur Bark will soon go home. He does not like going back to his apartment. He does not like anything much any more, in actual fact, apart from smoking, because that reminds him of the friend he has lost. Then he takes out his pack of cigarettes, taps the bottom, removes one, slips it between his lips, lights it, closes his eyes, and inhales the first puff.

And suddenly, as the menthol-flavoured smoke spreads through his body, as he sits in the darkness with his eyelids closed, he hears a voice in the distance, very far away, as if it were coming from another world, and the voice is calling out "Good-day! Good-day!" Monsieur Bark shudders. He opens his eyes. It is the voice of his friend. He recognises it.

"Good-day! Good-day!" the voice continues. Monsieur Bark is on his feet. He rushes about like a madman, spinning round in every direction, trying to discover where the voice is loudest or closest, in spite of the blaring of endless horns that try to drown it. Monsieur Bark's heart is thumping. That's him! There, close by, thirty yards away, twenty possibly, is Monsieur Tao-laï, strangely dressed in a blue dressing gown, gazing at him as he steps forward, one arm outstretched, a smile illuminating his wizened old face: "Good-day! Good-day!" The old man is walking towards him. Monsieur Bark runs to the edge of the pavement. He is so happy. He calls out, "Stay there, Monsieur Tao-laï! Don't move! Watch out for the cars!", for in his joy and his exhaustion, the old man has forgotten about the road, the traffic, the motorbikes, the lorries, the buses that skim past him, that break and avoid him at the last moment. He walks on, beaming, as one might walk on a cloud or on the surface of a lake.

Monsieur Linh sees his friend the fat man coming towards him. He can see him clearly now. He can hear his voice bidding him good-day. The old man says to *Sang diû*: "I told you we would find him again. There he is. How wonderful!"

For all Monsieur Bark's cries, his friend does not seem to hear him. He is still walking towards him. He is smiling. The two men are no more than ten yards from one another. They can see each other's face, each other's eyes, close to, and within each other's eyes the happiness at seeing themselves again.

But all of a sudden, like a never-ending scene in slow motion,

Monsieur Linh sees the expression on his friend's face change, freeze, and his mouth open. He can see him shouting, but he does not hear his shout because a deafening noise drowns out all other sounds. The old man hears the roar coming closer to him. He turns round, notices the car that is speeding towards him, skidding as it breaks; the contorted face of its driver, his hands clutching his wheel; he can read the fear in his eyes as well as a feeling of total helplessness. The old man protects his little girl as best he can, he puts his arms around her, he covers her with his body like a suit of armour; it goes on and on.

There is no end to it: the silent howl of his friend the fat man whom he is gazing at once more and at whom he is smiling; the horizontal lurch of the car hurtling towards him at full speed; the features of the driver, twisted in horror. Time stretches on, endlessly. Monsieur Linh is not afraid, he is no longer tired, he has seen his friend again, the weather is fine, his only concern is to protect his child as best he can, he hums the first words of the song to her, the car is close by, the little girl opens her eyes and looks at him, the old man kisses her forehead and then in his mind's eye all the beloved faces return to him, and in his memory there is the smell of the soil of his homeland, and the smell of the water, the smell of the forest, the smell of the sky and of the fire, the smell of the animals, the flowers and the hides, all the smells drawn together at last, at the moment that the car hits him, when he is thrown several yards, when he feels no pain, when he is huddled around the little body of *Sang diû*, when his head strikes the ground, sharply. And when, all of a sudden, it is night.

Monsieur Bark feels a violent chill run through his entire being. He remains transfixed for a few seconds, seeing the accident once more in his mind's eye, Monsieur Tao-laï's smile, the car looming up on him, careering violently into him despite the brakes being applied, the collision, the old man being tossed into the air and landing heavily on the ground with a noise like breaking wood.

Monsieur Bark shudders. Passers-by are already gathering round the body. The driver of the car still sits aghast in his car. Monsieur Bark rushes over, he brushes aside the curious onlookers, forces his way through the crowd, waving his arms furiously. He finally reaches his friend. The old man is lying curled up on his side. The blue dressing gown that is spread here and there over parts of his body resembles the corolla of an enormous flower. Powdery black earth seeps from a small, torn cloth bag beside him. There is also a photograph that has probably fallen out of a pocket, which Monsieur Bark recognises.

He falls to his knees. He picks up the photograph. He wants to take his friend in his arms, to speak to him, to tell him to hold on, that the emergency services are coming, that they will take him away and look after him and make him better, and that soon they will be able to go on their walks together again, and go to the restaurant, to the seaside, to the countryside, that they will never leave one another, ever again, he swears.

Monsieur Tao-laï's eyes are closed. Some blood is flowing from his head, from an invisible wound at the back of his skull. The blood follows the gradient of the road, like a faltering stream which then separates into five distinct trickles: it looks like the outline of a hand and its fingers and thumb. Monsieur Bark watches this fluctuating hand which his friend's life has formed, his life that is ebbing away. Curiously, as he gazes at this picture which Monsieur Tao-laï's blood is mapping out on the asphalt, he has a vague memory of a dream he had a few nights ago, a dream about a forest, a spring, an evening at dusk, cool water and oblivion.

Monsieur Bark lays his hand on the old man's shoulder as he so often used to do. It remains there for a long while. A very long while. Nobody dares to disturb him. Then, slowly, he gets to his feet at last. People stare at him, searchingly. They draw back and it is just at the moment that one of them steps backwards, rather as one steps back in the presence of someone better looking and more resplendent than oneself, that Monsieur Bark notices, lying at the man's feet, *Sans dieu*, the pretty doll that his friend Monsieur

Tao-laï would never be parted from, constantly lavishing his attention on her, as if she were a real child. Monsieur Bark's heart leaps when he sees the doll with her beautiful black hair. She is wearing the dress which he had given to his friend for her. Her eyes are wide open. She is unscathed. Not a scratch. It is as if she seems just slightly surprised, and that she is waiting.

The fat man bends over and picks her up carefully. "*Sans dieu*," he murmurs in her ear, smiling in spite of the tears that are starting to blur his gaze. Then he turns towards his friend and lays the doll on his chest. The blood has stopped flowing. Monsieur Bark closes his eyes. He suddenly feels very tired, more tired than he has ever been. He keeps his eyes closed. He no longer wants to open them. The night is very soothing, and he stares into his own darkness. It feels good there. If only it could last. If only it would never end.

"*Sang diû . . . Sang diû . . .*"

Monsieur Bark's eyes are still closed.

"*Sang diû . . . Sang diû . . .*"

He can hear the voice, but he tells himself it must be a dream. And he does not want to leave this dream.

"*Sang diû . . . Sang diû . . .*"

The voice does not stop. On the contrary, it grows louder. And more joyful too. Monsieur Bark opens his eyes. Close beside him, the old man looks at him and smiles. He is clasping *Sans dieu* in his arms, stroking her hair with one hand while his other hand reaches eagerly towards his friend. He tries to raise his head.

"Don't move, Monsieur Tao-laï! Whatever you do, don't move," shouts Monsieur Bark, who lets out a great laugh, a laugh as huge as he is, and which he is unable to control. "The emergency services are on their way. Keep still!"

The old man has understood. He lets his head fall back gently onto the asphalt. The fat man takes his hand. The hand suffuses a pleasant warmth through him. Monsieur Bark feels he wants to embrace all these people who are gathered around, all these strangers whom he would like to have murdered a few moments ago. His friend is alive. Alive! So life can also be like this, he thinks. Miracles can sometimes happen, and there can be riches, and laughter, and hope once more just when you think that everything around you is nothing but destruction and silence.

Dusk is falling. The sky is the colour of milk; a dark and soothing milk. *Sang diû* rests lightly on Monsieur Linh's chest. He has the feeling that she is giving him her youthful vigour. He can feel himself coming back to life. No wretched car is going to get the better of him. He has experienced famines and wars. He has crossed oceans. He is invincible. He puts his lips to the little girl's forehead. He has found his friend again. He smiles at the fat man. He says good-day to him several times. Monsieur Bark replies "good-day, good-day", and these repeated words become like a song, a song for two voices.

The emergency services arrive and bustle around the injured man, whom they place with the utmost care on a stretcher. The old man does not appear to be in pain. The stretcher bearers carry him to the ambulance. Monsieur Bark holds his hand as he talks to him. It is the beginning of a very beautiful springtime; the very beginning. The old man looks at his friend and smiles at him. He hugs the pretty doll in his scrawny arms, he hugs her as if his life depended on her; he hugs her as he would hug a real child, quiet, calm and eternal, a child of the dawn and of the east.

His one and only child.

Monsieur Linh's grand-daughter.